THE PRIMROSE

THE DESERT ISLAND DRACULA LIBRARY
promotes the study of Dracula, vampirism, and the works of Bram Stoker

DRACULA: THE SHADE AND THE SHADOW
Edited by Elizabeth Miller   1-874287-10-4

DRACULA UNEARTHED
Annotated by Clive Leatherdale   1-874287-12-0

DRACULA: THE NOVEL AND THE LEGEND —
A STUDY OF BRAM STOKER'S GOTHIC MASTERPIECE
Clive Leatherdale   1-874287-04-X

THE ORIGINS OF DRACULA — THE BACKGROUND
TO BRAM STOKER'S GOTHIC MASTERPIECE
Clive Leatherdale   1-874287-07-4

TREATISE ON VAMPIRES AND REVENANTS —
THE PHANTOM WORLD
Dissertation on those Persons who Return
to Earth Bodily, the Excommunicated, the
Oupires or Vampires, Vroucolacas, &c
Dom Augustine Calmet   1-874287-06-6

THE JEWEL OF SEVEN STARS
Annotated by Clive Leatherdale   1-874287-08-2

THE LADY OF THE SHROUD
Annotated by William Hughes   1-874287-22-8

THE PRIMROSE PATH
Introduced by Richard Dalby   1-874287-21-X

The Primrose Path

by

BRAM STOKER

INTRODUCED BY
RICHARD DALBY

Desert Island Books

First Published in 1999

DESERT ISLAND BOOKS
89 Park Street, Westcliff-on-Sea, Essex SS0 7PD
United Kingdom
www.users.globalnet.co.uk/~desert

British Library Cataloguing-in-Publication Data
A catalogue record for this book is available from
the British Library

ISBN 1-874287-21-X

Printed in Great Britain
by
Redwood Books, Trowbridge, Wiltshire

Contents

INTRODUCTION

'Do not, as some ungracious pastors do,
Show me the steep and thorny way to heaven,
Whiles, liked a puffed and reckless libertine,
Himself the primrose path of dalliance treads,
And recks not his own rede.'

Hamlet, Act I, Scene 3

Like many authors and actors, Bram Stoker served a long apprenticeship, honing his youthful talents for over ten years in his native Dublin, before settling permanently in London as general factotum, assistant, and 'acting manager' to Henry Irving for twenty-six years.

During the 1870s, while maintaining his routine day-job in the Civil Service in Dublin Castle, Stoker wrote innumerable editorials and news items for *The Irish Echo* and *The Halfpenny Press,* and theatrical notices and longer reviews for the *Dublin Mail*, besides occasional pieces of sensational and imaginative fiction, in *The Shamrock* and *The Warder.*

These were entirely forgotten until Harry Ludlam first mentioned (in *A Biography of Dracula*, 1962) Stoker's 'hair-raising *Shamrock* cliff-hangers,' specifically 'his first horror venture': *The Chain of Destiny.*

It was not until I researched my own *Bibliography* of Bram Stoker in 1983 that the two earlier *Shamrock* serials – *The Primrose Path* and *Buried Treasures* – were first specifically named and described; but in the subsequent fifteen years they have both remained unread and neglected.

The third *Shamrock* yarn, *The Chain of Destiny*, is currently in print in *The Best Ghost and Horror Stories of Bram Stoker* (Dover, 1997) which I co-edited with S T Joshi and Stefan Dziemianowicz – but Stoker's first short novel, *The Primrose Path*, and its immediate successor *Buried Treasures*, have never been reprinted anywhere since their original fleeting and ephemeral magazine appearances in early 1875 until now.

I remain convinced (although it cannot be proved categorically) that the great Irish master of horror and mystery fiction Joseph Sheridan Le Fanu actively helped the young Stoker – in his very early days as a struggling tyro writer – to get his first weird tale, 'The Crystal Cup,' published in the prestigious monthly *London Society* magazine in September 1872, where the great novelist's cataleptic classic, *The Room in the Dragon Volant*, had been serialised earlier in the same year (February to June 1872).

After Le Fanu's untimely death in 1873, Stoker no longer had any prominent local literary champion to promote his fictional efforts. It is easy to imagine him furiously writing many more short stories and novellas for the bestselling London monthly and weekly magazines.

Having collected and read many of these 1870s magazines, notably *All the Year Round, Argosy, Belgravia, Cornhill, Cassell's, Quiver,* and *Temple Bar,* as well as *London Society,* I've usually found the majority of their serials and short stories (by once celebrated authors, most now far less well known than Stoker himself) unsurprisingly turgid, moralistic, and often badly written, and most are nowhere as good – or readable – as the stories contained in the present volume.

Over a hundred years ago there was a frequently repeated anecdote that 'Bram Stoker and two other young men at Trinity College, Dublin, decided to see who could compose the most ghastly story, and that Dracula was the only one of the three that was not too horrible to print!'

As a quarter-century separated his Trinity days and the writing of Dracula, the finale of this anecdote was probably misconstrued.

When this anecdote was quoted to Bram Stoker's widow (during an interview given in January 1927), she replied: 'The story you have in mind must have been a much earlier work. But, then, my husband was always writing horrible stories. When he was at work on *Dracula* we were all frightened of him. It was up on a lonely part of the east coast of Scotland, and he seemed to get obsessed by the spirit of the thing. There he would sit for hours, like a great bat, perched on the rocks of the shore or wander alone up and down the sandhills, thinking it out.'

It now seems very likely that the 'ghastly' story Stoker composed in his earlier Dublin days was really 'The Primrose Path' (if not 'The Chain of Destiny' which followed later).

I assume that *The Primrose Path*, with its intentionally vivid London setting, was aimed directly for English as well as Irish readers, but was obviously rejected by *London Society* and all other leading journals of the period.

Recently established at 33 Lower Abbey Street, Dublin, *The Shamrock* had quickly become a very popular magazine for the masses, with its self-publicised hype running as follows: 'Four Original Serial Stories and a Piece of Original Music now form the Chief Attractions of the SHAMROCK, for which the charge is but One Penny Weekly – a fact quite unprecedented in the History of Cheap Literature.'

Overall it was a superior version to the notorious 'penny dreadfuls' of the early and mid-nineteenth century (which had memorably carried such immortal seemingly endless cliffhanging mega-serials like *Varney the Vampyre*), and much closer in appearance to the later penny weeklies so popular in London during the 1880s and 1890s like *Titbits* and *Answers* (which serialised Richard Marsh's *The Beetle* under its original title of 'The Peril of Paul Lessingham: The Story of a Haunted Man' during the three months preceding the first edition of *Dracula*, in 1897).

The Primrose Path – billed as 'an entirely Original Story, specially written for the SHAMROCK, by A STOKER, Esq ... Beautifully Illustrated by an Eminent Artist' – ran for five weeks in Volume XII of *The Shamrock* from 6 February to 6 March 1875 (numbers 434 to 438); alongside another rousing serial, *The Irish-Americans; or, The Rival Heirs*, by the late General Charles G Halpine.

The five graphically-drawn illustrations form an integral and very important partnership with Stoker's text, especially the first allegorical picture of Death and the Devil which is specifically described in the second chapter, and is effectively the metaphorical core of the story and symbolic catalyst of the events that follow.

Although these illustrations are unsigned, they are most probably by Stoker's friend, and former Trinity colleague, the Reverend William Fitzgerald (a parish priest in Killaloe, County Clare), who later provided the major drawings for Stoker's *Under the Sunset* in 1881.

In this first picture, the skull-faced rider and the demon figure in peaked cap and 'long floating cloak' have decidedly horrific and underlying supernatural pre-*Dracula* overtones, before they metamorphose in reality as the sinister bar-keeper whose face 'resembled more the ghastly front of a skull than the face of a living man,' and the tall mesmeric Irving-like actor 'who was performing the part of "Mephistopheles".' (The two illustrations accompanying *Buried Treasures* – one of them bearing an inscription – appear to be by a different artist).

Many of the events in *The Primrose Path* are curiously prophetic, describing the aspirations and career of an Irishman (Jerry O'Sullivan) who is invited to work in a London theatre – just four years before Stoker himself followed the same course, albeit in a far more elevated position.

O'Sullivan is hired as the theatre's head carpenter, supervising the mechanism of the traps, enabling the rise of the demons from underground. His work is so intense that he keeps 'dreaming of slots, and flies, and wings, and flats, and vampire traps ...'

This novella is an obvious moral tract on the degradation and evils of alcoholism. The exemplary teetotaller Parnell (Stoker's own wishful self-identity of moral rectitude?) preaches against whisky and spirits of every kind – 'the curse of Ireland' – and London is described as 'a city where the devil lives, if he lives any one place in the world.'

Stoker appears to be urging his fellow countrymen to be content with their happy, if poverty-stricken, lot in Ireland, well loved and supported by their families and friends, rather than succumbing to the devilish temptation of false riches and excesses of London.

O'Sullivan's steady descent into Hell takes place as the terrible bar-keeper and Mephistophelian actor gradually coax him to imbibe whisky and beer, which had scarcely passed his lips in Ireland, and quickly leads to his first-ever bout of inebriation, with 'the drunkard's feeble maundering gape.'

As a regular toper, nearly always in a state of 'fuddle,' O'Sullivan is a daily inhabitant of 'that hell-cauldron, which is picturesquely termed "the bowl".'

The clearly signposted grisly climax to this tragic horror story comes as no surprise. As with the original climax of *The Jewel of Seven Stars* (1903; also published by Desert Island Books in an annotated edition, 1996), Stoker preferred the true-to-life realistic denouement, rather than a false happy ending.

Katey O'Sullivan shines throughout as the earliest example of Stoker's 'ideal woman,' Jerry's dutiful wife and saintly

'Guardian Angel.'

The Primrose Path stands out as one of the strongest anti-alcohol parables of the Victorian era, and it is quite surprising that none of the flourishing Christian publishers like the Religious Tract Society ever revived it for publication in book form.

It could be inferred that Stoker himself was an abstainer who never drank whisky or any strong alcohol of any kind, though undoubtedly he must have consumed untold gallons of wine during his nightly dinners with Irving and the company at the Beefsteak Room after the Lyceum productions. No records of overt drunkenness at these dinners have survived!

The success of *The Primrose Path* was great enough to encourage *The Shamrock* editor to commission another short serial from Stoker, *Buried Treasures*, for the two issues (13 and 20 March 1875) immediately following the first story.

Barely one year later Stoker had his first historic life-changing encounter with the mesmeric actor Henry Irving, which swiftly launched their enduring and unique partnership and control of the Lyceum company.

The Shamrock remains incredibly rare in any state, and complete runs are unknown outside the National Library of Ireland (in the splendid Joly Collection). The Bodleian and British Library only received isolated copies, excluding the Stoker stories. Special thanks are due to both Tom Francis and David Rowlands for locating and sending me copies of all *The Shamrock* stories in 1982, and also to John Moore, Albert Power and David Lass (Secretary of the Bram Stoker Society) for their additional assistance.

RICHARD DALBY

SERIES EDITOR'S NOTE

Bram Stoker's *The Primrose Path* is more than just a hitherto forgotten tale, published here for the first time since its weekly serialisation in the Dublin magazine *The Shamrock* in early 1875. Its timing sheds light on the author and his restricted circumstances.

Abraham Stoker (junior) was born on 8 November 1847. He was therefore just 27 when *The Primrose Path* appeared in print, under the name A Stoker, Esq. Publishing moves slowly, and when one takes into account the unavoidable pile of rejection slips, the interlude between writing and publication was likely to be many months, perhaps years. Stoker, in other words, probably wrote *The Primrose Path* when he was 25 or 26, or even younger.

A broad chronology of Stoker's life may be found in his *Personal Reminiscences of Henry Irving* (1906). The early chapters reveal that in 1875 the momentous events and influences of Stoker's adult life – his employment by Irving, his marriage to Florence Balcombe, and his uprooting from Dublin to London – were as yet undreamed of. In his mid-twenties Stoker was still a desk-bound bachelor toiling away as a junior civil servant in Dublin Castle.

His relationship with Irving is especially pertinent. Stoker saw the promising actor Henry Irving perform in Dublin in August 1867 (when Stoker was nineteen and Irving ten years older) and again in 1871. In Stoker's own words: 'More than five years elapsed before I saw Henry Irving again.' That was in December 1896, by which time the circumstances of both men had changed. Irving's was no longer a rising star; it shone as brightly as any in the theatrical world. And Stoker was no longer a mere punter; his love of the stage had prompted him to take on the (unpaid) duties of theatre critic for the *Dublin Mail*. As *The Primrose Path* demonstrates, Stoker was already intimate with the theatrical world, spending as much time backstage as before it. It was in his capacity as critic that he was now introduced to Irving, face to face, and the impact of that meeting set in train the upheavals that would shape Stoker's destiny. It was also around this time that his father died, prompting Abraham junior to assume the diminutive 'Bram' by which he was thenceforth known.

As the first meeting with Irving did not take place until almost two years after *The Primrose Path* was published, Stoker might have blushed at the memory of one particular passage. He had written: 'Amongst the actors was a tall individual who was performing the part of 'Mephistopheles,' ... he [Jerry O'Sullivan] did not like the appearance of his new friend.' Mephistopheles was one of Irving's favourite roles, and the allusion to the 'tall' actor is unlikely to have been coincidental. Stoker's unflattering reference is unlikely to have come back to haunt him. Unless the actor had occasion to delve into back issues of *The Shamrock* he would never have come across it.

With regard to Florence Balcombe, Stoker's wife-to-be, it is not known whether in 1875 they were acquainted. She was then just sixteen, and a year later was involved in a relationship of sorts with fellow Dubliner Oscar Wilde, seven years Stoker's junior. Florence's taste in men was, to say the least, eclectic. Where Wilde was Bohemian, Stoker appears to have been much more of a stick-in-the-mud, though this is contrary to what one often reads. 'Genial' is the adjective handed down over the years to describe Stoker's personality. Be this as it may, nothing in his voluminous writings suggests other than an uptight, generally humourless individual, someone with a penchant for censorious moralising and a sacrosanct regard for duty.

Nor are these traits discernable only in Stoker's 'mature' writings. His stern views on women, on alcohol, on the evils of the lower classes, are all manifest in *The Primrose Path*. If Florence entertained doubts about the unbending mentality of her future husband, she only had to open its pages to find the following authorial asides: 'Wives, be careful how you argue with your husbands,' and 'The analysis of a sensual nature shows two evil qualities.'

The couple married in December 1878, an event hastily brought forward in order that they might set up home in London, where Stoker had taken employment as business manager of Irving's Lyceum Theatre. Stoker would manage Irving's business until the actor's death in 1905.

There is something almost eerie in the way *The Primrose Path* anticipates Stoker uprooting himself from his homeland, almost as if it were a premonition of his own future. We know from *Personal Reminiscences* that in the 1870s he had undertaken several trips to London, either on vacation or as part of his Civil Service duties. The descriptions of coastal England in *The Primrose Path* show Stoker to have been personally familiar with the three-day sea voyage from Dublin around Cornwall, through the English Channel and up the Thames.

As Richard Dalby has pointed out in his introduction, only one published Stoker story, pre-*The Primrose Path*, has come to light – 'The Crystal Cup,' dating from 1872. Stoker, in other words, in his mid-twenties was but an aspiring writer, hardened to rejection. With no track record, he would have had to hawk his stories around magazines in London and Dublin. With little success, it would seem. It is a safe bet that many of Stoker's early works languished in drawers, never to be published.

Part of Stoker's difficulty was that he could not settle on a genre that best suited his talents. This problem would stay with him throughout his life. Though best known for *Dracula*, his output of eighteen books and innumerable short stories and articles may be sub-divided into romances, non-fiction, fairy tales, moralistic lectures, and, of course, horror. Horror-writing was just one string to his bow, and on the strength of *Dracula* the most estimable. But the young Stoker did not yet know this. Lacking originality and insight – let alone the bookish background knowledge that was a prerequisite for a mature work like *Dracula* – he turned his hand to anything he thought might get published.

The Primrose Path cannot be classified as a horror tale, but that is not to say that elements of *Dracula* cannot be discerned within it. Not the least surprising reference in its pages is to 'vampire traps.' But one also finds numerous turns of phrase, motifs, quirks, casts of mind, fledgling ideas that would later be repeated or expanded in other works, notably *Dracula*. *The Primrose Path*, for example, shows Stoker's liking for the adjectives 'hearty,' 'man-like' and 'woman-like,' and for detailed place settings around a table. We find the idea of one man in ten paying his dues, later applied to Dracula at the devil's academy. London, Stoker wrote, long before Dracula's invasion, is 'a city where the devil lives.' Nor can he resist long passages of near-incomprehensible dialect, with idiosyncratic and inconsistent mis-spellings, the blame for which in most readers' minds probably rests with the type-setters.

Young Stoker is already alive to the potential of blurred identity ('She knew the step that was her husband's, and yet not his.') and temporary remission from attack (he 'was quite his old self') before the final onslaught commences.

There can be between husband and wife no secrets, as Mina will later explain in *Dracula*. In both tales men suffer 'brain fever,' beside whose bed a dutiful wife waits patiently; and in both a grieving partner pushes the other away amid accusations of infidelity: 'Oh, Jerry ... that ever the day should come when you should put me from you.' 'What have I done to deserve all this.'

Jerry O'Sullivan, the central character in *The Primrose Path*, suffers horrid dreams, senses he is going mad, feels possessed by a demon force, laughs the hard, cold laugh of a demon, and attacks those dearest to him – all themes revisited in *Dracula*. And the Count himself will later utter almost the very words that pass from another's lips: 'I will be revenged on you.'

Extending to 32,000 words, *The Primrose Path* is too long to be properly considered a short story, and too brief to be treated as a novel. It is, however, by some way the most substantial piece of fiction penned by Stoker prior to *The Snake's Pass*, published fifteen years later in 1890.

Buried Treasures, the second of Stoker's stories presented here to the reader, is an altogether shorter and lighter tale. At fewer than 8,000 words, it allows Stoker room only to revisit the well-trodden path of sunken ships and treasure chests. *Buried Treasures* is valuable less in itself than for its signposts to future Stoker novels. This time the moralising takes Christian form. Apropos of nothing, Stoker describes Christmas as 'the greatest of all Christian festivals ... which is kept all over the world, wherever the True Light has fallen.'

Buried Treasures is set in Dollymount near Clontarf, Stoker's birthplace, just north of Dublin. His description of storms at sea prefigures the epic destruction in *Dracula* of the vessel Demeter at Whitby. The object of the heroes' attention – prising open a mysterious iron chest – anticipates the 'coffins,' 'boxes,' 'chests,' 'safes' and 'sarcophagi' to be found in *Dracula* (1897), *The Mystery of the Sea* (1902), *The Jewel of Seven Stars* (1903) and *The Lair of the White Worm* (1911).

CLIVE LEATHERDALE
Series Editor

The Primrose Path

1

A Happy Home

'I wonder will any of them come, Jerry?'
The pretty little woman's face got puckered all over with baby wrinkles, more suitable to the wee pink face that lay on her bosom than to her own somewhat pale one, as she made the remark.

Jerry looked up from his newspaper and gazed at her lovingly for a moment before he answered, his answer being a confident smile with a knowing shake of the head from side to side as who should say – 'Oh, you little humbug, pretending to distress yourself with doubts. Of course, they'll come – all of them.'

Katey seemed to lose her trouble in his smile – it is wonderful what comforters love and sympathy are. She drew close to her husband and held down the tiny bald pink head for him to kiss, and then, leaning her cheek against his, said in a soft cooing voice, half wifely, half motherly, 'Oh, Jerry, isn't he a little beauty.'

Children are quite as jealous as dogs and cats in their own way, and instinctively the urchin sprawling on the hearth-rug came over and pulled at his mother's dress, saying plaintively 'Me too, mammy – me too.'

Jerry took the child on his knee. 'Eh, little Jerry, your nose is out of joint again; isn't it?'

A mother is jealous as well as her child, and this mother answered – 'Oh, no, Jerry, sure I don't love him less because I have to take care of the little mite.'

Further conversation was stopped by a knock at the door.

'That's some of them stayin' away,' said Jerry, as he went out to open the door.

As may be seen, Jerry and his wife expected company, the doubts as to whose arrival was caused by the extreme inclemency of the weather, and as the occasion of the festivities was an important one, the doubts were strong.

Jerry O'Sullivan was a prosperous man in his line of life. His trade was that of a carpenter, and as he had, in addition to large practical skill and experience gained from unremitting toil, a considerable share of natural ability, was justly considered by his compeers to be the makings of a successful man.

Three years before he had been married to his pretty little wife, whose sweet nature, and care for his comfort, and whose desire to perfect the cheerfulness of home, had not a little aided his success, and kept him on the straight path.

If every wife understood the merits which a cheerful home has above all other places in the eyes of an ordinary man, there would be less brutality than there is amongst husbands, and less hardships and suffering amongst wives.

The third child has just been christened, and some friends and relatives were expected to do honour to the occasion, and now the knock announced the first arrival.

Whilst Jerry went to the door, Katey arranged the child's garments so as to make him look as nice as possible, and also fixed her own dress, somewhat disturbed by maternal cares. In the meantime little Jerry flattened his nose against the window pane in a vain desire to see the appearance of the first arrival. Little Katey stood by him looking expectant as though her eyes were with her brother's.

Mrs Jerry's best smile showed that the newcomer, Mr Parnell, was a special friend. After shaking hands with him she stood close to him, and showed him the baby, looking up into his dark strong face with a smile of perfect trust. He was so tall that he had to stoop to kiss the baby, although the little mother raised it in her arms for him. He said very tenderly –

'Let me hold him a minute in my arms.'

He lifted him gently as he spoke, and bending his head, said reverently: –

'God bless him. Suffer little children to come unto me, for of such is the kingdom of Heaven.'

Katey's eyes were full of tears as she took him back, and she thanked the big man with a look too full of sacred feeling for even a smile.

Jerry stood by in silence. He felt much, although he did not know what to say.

Another knock was heard, and again Jerry's services were required. This time there was a large influx, for three different bodies had joined just at the door. Much laughter was heard in the hall, and then they all entered. The body consisted of seven souls all told.

Place aux dames. We Irishmen must give first place always to the ladies. Of these there were four. Jerry's mother and her assistant, Miss M'Anaspie, and Katey's two sisters, one older and one younger than herself. The men were, Mr Muldoon, Tom Price, and Patrick Casey.

Jerry's mother was a quiet dignified old lady, very gentle in manner, but with a sternness of thought and purpose which shone through her gentleness and forbid any attempt at imposition, as surely as the green light marks danger at a railway crossing. She had a small haberdashery shop, by which she was reputed amongst her friends to have realised a considerable amount of money. Miss M'Anaspie was her assistant, and was asked by Katey to be present out of pure kindness. She had originally set her cap at Jerry, and had very nearly succeeded in her aim. It was no small evidence of Katey's genuine goodness of nature and her perfect trust of her husband that she was present; for most women have a feeling of possible hostility, or, at least, maintain an armed neutrality towards the former flames of the man that they love. Miss M'Anaspie was tall and buxom, and of lively manners, quite devoid of bashfulness. It puzzled many of her friends how, with her desire to be married, she had not long ago succeeded in accomplishing her wish. Katey's sisters were pleasant, quiet girls, both engaged to be married – Jane to Price, and Mary to Casey, the former man being a blacksmith, and the latter an umbrella-maker, both being sturdy young fellows, and looking forward to being shortly able to marry.

Mr Muldoon was the great man of the occasion. He was a cousin of Mrs O'Sullivan's, and was rich. He had a large Italian warehouse, which he managed well, and consequently was exceedingly prosperous. Personally he was not so agreeable as he might have been. He was small, and stout, and ugly, with keen eyes, a sharply-pointed nose; was habitually clean-shaven, and kept his breast stuck out like that of a pouter pigeon. He always dressed gorgeously, and on the present occasion, as he considered that he was hon-ouring his poor relations, had got himself up to a pitch of such radiance that his old servant had commented on his appearance as he had left home. His trousers were of the lightest yellow whipcord; his coat was blue; his waistcoat was red velvet, with blue glass buttons; and in the matter of green tie, high collar, and large cuffs he excelled. His watch chain, of massive gold, with the 'pint of seals' attached to the fob-chain after the manner of the bucks of the last genera-tion was alone worthy of respect. His temper was not pleas-ant, for he was dictatorial to the last degree, and had a very unpleasant habit, something like Frederick the Great, of considering any difference of opinion as an insult intention-ally offered to himself.

A man like this may be a pleasant enough companion so long as he goes with the tide, he thinking that it is the tide which goes with him; but when occasion of difference arises, the social horizon at once becomes overcast with angry clouds which gather quickly till the storm has burst. Often-times, as in nature – the great world of elements – the storm clears the air.

Mr Muldoon had been asked as an act possibly likely to benefit the new olive branch, for the Italian grocer was unmarried, and might at some future time, so thought Jerry and Katey in their secret hearts, take in charge the destinies of the new infant to-day made John Muldoon O'Sullivan.

When the party entered the room Mr Muldoon had advanced to Mrs Jerry, and, as she was a pretty little woman, had kissed her in a semi-paternal way which made Miss M'Anaspie giggle. Mr Muldoon looked round half indignantly, for he felt that his dignity was wounded. He considered that Miss M'Anaspie, of whose very name he was ignorant, was a forward young person, and in his mind determined to let her understand so before the evening was over.

After a few minutes the introductions had all been accomplished, and everybody knew everybody else. There was great kissing of the baby, great petting of the two elder children, for whose delectation sundry sweets were produced from mysterious pockets, and much laughter and good-humoured jesting.

Mr Muldoon prided himself upon being a good hand at saying smart things, and felt that the present occasion was not one to be thrown away. Being a bachelor, he considered that his most proper attitude was that of ignorance – utter ignorance regarding babies in general, and this one in particular. When he was shown the baby he put up his eye-glass, and said:

'What is this?'

'Oh, Mr Muldoon,' said the mother, almost reproachfully. 'Sure, don't you know this is the new baby?'

'Oh! oh! indeed. It is very bald.'

'It won't be long so, then,' interrupted Miss M'Anaspie pertly. 'You can make it your *heir,* if you will.' Her English method of aspiration pointed the joke.

Mr Muldoon looked at her almost savagely, but said nothing. He did not want to commit himself to any intention of aiding the child's career; and he was obliged to remain silent. He mentally scored another black mark against the speaker.

Presently he spoke again.

'Is it a boy or a girl?'

'A boy.'

'And are these boys or girls?' He pointed as he spoke to little Jerry and little Katey.

Miss M'Anaspie answered again – 'Neither. They are half of each.'

'Dear me,' said Mr Muldoon. 'Can that be?'

'Don't you see,' said Miss M'Anaspie in a tone which implied the addition of the words 'you silly old fool,' 'one is a boy and the other a girl.'

Mr Muldoon made another black mark in his mental note-book, and ignoring his opponent, as he already considered Miss M'Anaspie, spoke again to Katey.

'And are these all yours? Three children; and you have been married – let me see, how long?'

'Three years and two months.'

'Why, at this rate, what will you do in twenty years. Just fancy twenty children. Really, Mrs Katey, you should take the pledge.'

Katey did not know what to answer, and so stayed silent. Miss M'Anaspie turned away to hide an imagined blush, and Mr Muldoon feeling that he had said something striking, began to unbend and mix with the rest of the company in a better humour than he had been in for some time.

The table was ready set with all the materials for comfort, and as the teapot was basking inside the fender beside a dish of highly buttered cake, the work of Mrs Jerry herself, and the kettle singing songs of a bacchanalian character on the fire, promise of comfort to the foes and friends of Father Mathew was not wanting.

There was great arranging of places at the table. Jane and Mary with their sweethearts managed to monopolise one entire side, sitting alternately like the bread and ham in the pile of sandwiches before them.

Mr Muldoon was put next to Katey, and Jerry had his mother on his right hand, she being supported on the other side by Mr Parnell. This left Miss M'Anaspie to take her seat without choice, between the two eldest men of the party.

She did not shrink from the undertaking, however, but sat down, saying pertly to the company, but to no one in particular –

'My usual luck. Never mind. I like to have an old man on each side of me.'

Mr Muldoon liked to be thought young – most middle-aged bachelors do – and he looked his disapprobation of the remark so strongly that a silence fell on all.

The dowager Mrs O'Sullivan said quietly –

'You let your tongue run too fast, Margaret. You forget Mr Muldoon is a new friend of yours, and not an old one.'

Miss M'Anaspie had already seen that she had made a mistake, and was only waiting for an opportunity of correcting it, so she seized it greedily.

'I am so awfully sorry. I hope, sir, I did not offend. Indeed I wished to please. I thought that young people wished to be thought old. I know that I did when I was young.'

'That was some time ago,' whispered Pat Casey to Mary,

who laughed too suddenly, and was nearly caught at it.

Mr Muldoon was mollified. He thought to himself that
perhaps the poor girl did not mean to give offence; that she
was a clever girl; much nicer after all than most girls; however that he would have an eye on her, and see what she was
like.

For some time the consumption of the good things occupied the attention of everybody. Mrs Jerry handed a cup of
tea to Mr Parnell before any of the rest of the men, saying –

'I know you like that better than anything else.'

'That I do,' he answered heartily. 'There is as much virtue
in this as there is evil in beer, and whisky, and gin, and all
other abominations.'

No one felt inclined to take up, at present at all events,
the total-abstinence glove thus thrown down, and so the
subject dropped.

It would have done one good to have seen the care which
Katey's sisters took of their sweethearts, piling up their
plates with everything that was nice, and keeping them as
steadily at work as if they had been engaged in a contest as
to who should consume the largest quantity in the smallest
time. This was a species of friendly rivalry in which the men
found equal pleasure with the girls.

It is quite wonderful the difference between the appetites
of successful and unsuccessful lovers.

Mr Muldoon and Miss M'Anaspie during the progress of
the meal became fast friends, at least so it would seem, for
they bandied, unchecked, pleasantries of a nature usually
only allowed amongst intimate friends. Both Jerry and his
wife were much amazed, for both stood somewhat in awe of
the great man with whom they would never have attempted
to make any familiarity.

By the time the heavy part of the eating was done, the
whole assemblage was in hearty good humour.

Katey began to clear away the things, having given the
baby in charge to her mother-in-law. The moment she began,
however, Mary and Jane started up and insisted that they
should do the work, and on her showing signs of determination forced her into the arm-chair, and placed the two sweethearts on guard over her, threatening them with various

pains and penalties in event of their failing in their trust.

Seeing the other girls at work, Miss M'Anaspie insisted on helping also, and they were too kind-hearted not to make her welcome in the little kindly office.

The next addition to the working staff was Mr Muldoon, who, to the astonishment of every one who knew him, clamoured loudly for work, evidently bent on going wherever Miss M'Anaspie went, and on helping her in her every task.

It was a sight to see the great man work. He evidently felt that he was extending and being more friendly with his inferiors than, perhaps, in justice to his own position he was warranted in doing; and he took some pains to let every one see that he was playing at work. His ignorance of the simplest domestic offices was preternatural. He did not know how to carry even a plate without putting it somewhere he ought not, or spilling its contents over some one; and he managed to break a tumbler and two plates just to show, like Beaumarchais and the watch, that that sort of thing was not in his line.

Mrs Jerry did not know Pope's lines about the perfection of a woman's manner and temper, wherein he puts as the culmination of her virtues,

'And mistress of herself though china fall;'

but she had the good temper and the good manner of nature, which is above all art, and although, woman-like, the wreck of her household goods went to her heart, she said nothing, but looked as sweet as if the breakage pleased her.

Truly, Jerry O'Sullivan had a sweet wife and a happy home. Prosperity seemed to be his lot in life.

2

To and Fro

When all was made comfortable for the after sitting, the conversation grew lively. The position of persons at table tends to further cliquism, and to narrow conversation to a number of dialogues, and so the change was appreciated.

The most didactic person of the company was Mr Parnell, who was also the greatest philosopher; and the idea of general conversation seemed to have struck him. He began to comment on the change in the style of conversation.

'Look what a community of feeling does for us. Half an hour ago, when we were doing justice to Mrs O'Sullivan's good things, all our ideas were scattered. There was, perhaps, enough of pleasant news amongst us to make some of us happy, and others of us rich, if we knew how to apply our information; but still no one got full benefit, or the opportunity of full benefit, from it.'

Here Price whispered something in Jane's ear, which made her blush and laugh, and tell him to 'go along.'

Parnell smiled and said gently –

'Well, perhaps, Tom, some of the thoughts wouldn't interest the whole of us.'

Tom grinned bashfully, and Parnell reverted to his theme. He was a great man at meetings, and liked to talk, for he knew that he talked well.

'Have any of you ever looked how some rivers end?'

'What end?' asked Mr Muldoon, and winked at Miss M'Anaspie.

'The sea end. Look at the history of a river. It begins by a lot of little streams meeting together, and is but small at first. Then it grows wider and deeper, till big ships mayhap can sail in it, and then it goes down to the sea.'

'Poor thing,' said Mr Muldoon, again winking at Margaret.

'Ay, but how does it reach the sea? It should go, we would fancy, by a broad open mouth that would send the ships out boldly on every side and gather them in from every point. But some do not do so – the water is drawn off through a hundred little channels, where the mud lies in shoals and the sedges grow, and where no craft can pass. The river of thought should be an open river – be its craft few or many – if it is to benefit mankind.'

Miss M'Anaspie who had, whilst he was speaking, been whispering to Mr Muldoon, said, with a pertness bordering on snappishness:

'Then, I suppose, you would never let a person talk except in company. For my part, I think two is better company than a lot.'

'Not at all, my dear. The river of thought can flow between two as well as amongst fifty; all I say is that all should benefit.'

Here Mr Muldoon struck in. He had all along felt it as a slight to himself that Parnell should have taken the conversational ball into his own hands. He was himself extremely dogmatic, and no more understood the difference between didacticism and dogmatism than he comprehended the meaning of that baphometic* fire-baptism which set the critics of Mr Carlyle's younger days a-thinking.

'For my part,' said he, 'I consider it an impertinence for any man to think that what he says must be interesting to every one in a room.'

This was felt by all to be a home thrust at Parnell, and no one spoke. Parnell would have answered, not in anger, but in good-humoured argument, only for an imploring look on Katey's face, which seemed to say as plainly as words –

'Do not answer. He will be angry, and there will only be a quarrel.'

And so the subject dropped.

The men mixed punch, all except Mr Muldoon, who took his whisky cold, and Parnell, who took none. The former looked at the latter with a sort of semi-sneer, and said –

'Do you mean to say you don't take either punch or grog?'

---

* baphometic – worship of Baphomet, idol of the Knights Templar.

'Well,' said Parnell, 'I didn't mean to say it, but now that you ask me I do say it. I never touch any kind of spirit, and, please God, I never will.'

'Don't you think,' said Muldoon, 'that that is setting yourself above the rest of us a good deal. We're not too good for our liquor, but you are. That's about the long and the short of it.'

'No, no, my friend, I say nothing of the kind. Any man is too good for liquor.'

Jerry thought the conversation was getting entirely too argumentative, so he cut in –

'But a little liquor needn't be bad for a chap if he doesn't take too much?'

'Ay, there it is,' said Parnell, 'if he doesn't take too much. But he does take too much, and the end is that it works his ruin, body and soul.'

'Whose?'

It was Miss M'Anaspie who asked the question, and it fell like a bombshell.

Parnell, however, was equal to the emergency.

'Whose?' he repeated. 'Whose? Everyone's who begins and doesn't know where he may leave off.'

Miss M'Anaspie felt that she was answered, and looked appealingly at Mr Muldoon, who at once came to the rescue.

'Everyone is a big word. Do you mean to tell me that every man that drinks a pint of beer or a glass of whisky, goes straight to the devil?'

'No, no; indeed I do not. God forbid that I should say any such thing. But look how many men that mean only to take one glass, are persuaded to take two, and then the wits begin to go, and they take three or four, and five, ay, and more, sometimes. Why, men and women' – he rose from his chair as he spoke, with his face all aglow, with earnestness and belief in his words, 'look around you and see the misery that everywhere throngs the streets. See the pale, drunken, wasted-looking men, with sunken eyes, and slouching gait. Men that were once as strong and hard-working, and upright as any here, ay, and could look you in the face as boldly as any here. Look at them now! Afraid to meet your eyes, trembling at every sound; mad with passion one moment and with despair the next.'

The tide of his thought was pouring forth with such energy that no one spoke; even Mr Muldoon was afraid at the time to interrupt him. He went on:

'And the women, too, God help us all. Look at them and see what part drink plays in their wretched lives. Listen to the laughter and the cries that wake the echoes in the streets at night. You that have wives, and mothers and,' (this with a glance at Tom and Pat) 'sweethearts, can you hear such laughter and cries and not shudder? If you can, then when next you hear it think of what it would be for you to hear some voice that you love raised like *that*.'

Mr Muldoon could not stand it any longer and spoke out:

'But come now, I can't see how all the misery and wretchedness of the world is to be laid on a simple glass of beer.'

'Hear, hear,' said Miss M'Anaspie.

Parnell's reply was allegorical. 'Do you see how the oak springs from the acorn – the bird from the egg? I tell you that if there were no spirits there would be less sin, and shame, and sorrow than there is.'

'Oh, yes,' said Muldoon. 'It would be a beautiful world entirely, and everybody would have everything, and nobody would want nothing, and we'd all be grand fellows. Eh, Miss Margaret, what do you think?'

'Hear, hear,' said Miss M'Anaspie, more timidly than before, however, at the same time looking over at Mrs O'Sullivan, who was looking not too well pleased at her.

'Ah, sir,' said Parnell, sadly, 'God knows that we, men and women, are not what we ought to be, and sin will be in the world, I suppose, till the time that is told. But this I say, that drink is the greatest enemy that man has on earth.'

'Why, you're quite an enthusiast,' said Mr Muldoon; 'one would think you were inspired.'

'I would I were inspired. I wish my voice was of gold, and that I could make men hear me all over the world, and that I could make the stars ring again with cries against the madness that men bring upon themselves.'

'Upon my life,' said Mr Muldoon, 'you should be on the stage. You have missed your vocation. By the way, what is your vocation?'

'I am a hatter.'

Miss M'Anaspie blurted out suddenly, 'Mad as a hatter,' and then suddenly got red in the face, and shut up completely as she saw her employer's eye fixed on her with a glare almost baleful in its intensity.

Mr Muldoon laughed loudly, and slapped his fat knees as he ejaculated – 'Brayvo, brayvo. One for his nob – mad as a hatter. That accounts for the enthusiasm.' Then, seeing a look of such genuine pain on Katey's face that even his obtuseness could not hide from him how deeply he was hurting her, added – 'Of course, Mr Parnell, I am only joking; but still it is not bad – mad as a hatter. Ha, ha!'

No one said anything more, and no one laughed; and so the matter was dropped.

Jerry felt that a gloom had fallen on the assemblage, and tried to lift it by starting a new topic.

'Do you know,' said he, 'I had a letter from John Sebright the other day, and he tells me if you want to make money England's the place.'

'Indeed,' said his mother, satirically.

Going to England was an old 'fad' of Jerry's, and one which had caused his mother many an anxious hour of thought, and many a sleepless night.

'Yes,' answered Jerry, 'he says there is more work there than here, and better paid; and that a man has ten chances for gettin' on for one he has here.'

'The one chance often wins when the ten fail,' said Parnell.

'And it's worse losing ten pounds than one,' added Margaret.

'And some girls' tongues are as long as ten,' said Mrs O'Sullivan, who could not bear anything which tended to make light of her wishes with regard to Jerry, and so determined to put a stop to Miss M'Anaspie's volubility.

Mr Muldoon, however, came to the rescue.

'And some girls who have been for ten years in misery and discomfort find sometimes that one year brings them all they want.'

Miss M'Anaspie put her handkerchief before her face, and again dead silence fell on the assembly. Parnell broke it.

'Jerry, put the idea out of your head. You know that you couldn't go now even if you wanted, and there is no use sighing for what can't be.'

'I don't know that,' said Jerry argumentatively. 'I could go now with Katey and the young ones, just as well as if I was a boy still; ay, and better, for she would keep me out of harm.'

Parnell said with great feeling, 'That's right, Jerry; stick up for the wife and stick to her too, for she's worth it. Do you but keep to your wife, and the home that she will always make for you, as long as you let her, and you may go when and where you will, and your hands will find work.'

Katey began to cry. She was still a little delicate, and anything which touched her feelings upset her very much. There was an immediate rush of all the women in the room to comfort her.

Jerry offered her some of his punch, but she put the glass aside, saying –

'No, no, dear, I never take it.'

'Come, come,' said Mr Muldoon, 'Mrs Katey, this will never do, you must take it. It is good for you.'

'No, it is good for no one.'

'Come now, Mr Parnell,' said Mr Muldoon, 'don't you know a sup of liquor would do her good? Tell her so.'

'No, no,' said Katey, 'I know myself.'

Parnell spoke –

'I cannot say, but it is good as a medicine, and as a medicine one may take it without harm.'

'Capital thing to be sick sometimes,' said Muldoon, winking at Tom and Pat, and laughing at his own joke.

Parnell did not like to let a point go unquestioned on a subject on which he felt deeply, so he answered –

'When you are sick, your wish is to be well again, and the medicine that seems nice to you when well, is only in sickness but medicine after all.'

Once more Mr Muldoon began to get angry, and said, with a determination to fight the argument – *à l'outrance**–

'Why, man, you would make the world a hell with all your

---

*   *à l'outrance* – (French) to the bitter end of a combat.

DEATH AND DEVIL

self-denials. Do you think life would be worth having if every enjoyment of it, great and little, was to be suppressed. The world is bad enough, goodness knows, already, without making a regular hell of it.'

'Hell is a big word.'

'It is a big word, and I mean it to be a big word.'

'Ah, it is like enough to hell already,' said Parnell sadly.

'On account of all the bad spirits,' added Miss M'Anaspie.

'Laugh, my child. Laugh whilst you may. Heaven grant that the day may never come when you cannot laugh at such thoughts. Ay, truly, the world is hard enough as it is. Bad enough, and the devil is abroad enough, and too much.'

'Oh, he's on earth is he?'

'Yes, Mr Muldoon, he is, to and fro, he walks always.'

Whilst he was speaking he was drawing in his note-book.

Miss M'Anaspie got curious to know what he was doing, and asked him.

In reply he handed her the book.

She took it eagerly, and then passed it on to all the others in turn.

He had drawn an allegorical picture under which he had written – 'To and Fro.'

The picture represented a road through a moor to a village, seen lying some distance away, the spire of its church shadowed by a passing cloud. The moor was bleak, with, in the foreground, a clump of blasted trees, and in the distance a ruined house. On the road two travellers were journeying, both seated on the same horse – a sorry nag. One of them was booted and spurred, and wore a short cloak, a slouched hat, under which the lineaments showed ghastly, for the face was but that of a skull. The other, who rode pick-a-back, was clad as the German romances love to clothe their demon when he walks the earth, with trunk hose and pointed shoes, a long floating cloak, and peaked cap with cock's feathers. On his arm he bore a basket full of bottles, and as he clutched his grisly companion he laughed with glee, bending his head as men do when their enjoyment is in perspective rather than an actuality.

From beneath a stone a viper had raised itself, and seemed to salute the travellers with its forked tongue.

When the picture came into Mrs O'Sullivan's hands, she fixed her spectacles and held it up a little to let the most light possible fall on it. Then she spoke –

'God bless us and save us, but that's an awful thing. Where did you see that, Mr Parnell?'

'I never saw it, ma'am, except in my mind, and I see it there often enough. You, young men, mind the lesson of that picture, for it is truth. Death and the devil go together, and so sure as the devil grips hold of you, death is not far off, you may be sure, in some form or other, waiting, waiting, waiting.'

Mr Muldoon saw that the subject of drinking was coming in again, and said maliciously –

'And this is all from a glass of beer.'

'Ay, if you will,' said Parnell. 'That's how it begins – that which is the curse of Ireland in our own time; and which, so surely as Irishmen will not use the wit and strength that God has given them, will drag her from her throne.'

Jerry got into the conversation:

'One thing John Sebright tells me, that there is less

drunkenness in England than here.'

'Don't you believe him,' said Parnell. 'That man means mischief to you. He wants to entice you to England, and then live on you when he gets you there. For Heaven's sake put that idea of going away out of your head. You're very well here as you are; and let well alone.'

Jerry's mother spoke also. 'John Sebright is a nice chap to quote sobriety as a virtue. Do you remember how often I gave you money to pay his fines to keep him out of prison after his drunken freaks, for the sake of his poor dead and gone mother. Why, that chap could no more tell truth than he could work, and that's saying a good deal.'

'Well, drink or no drink, mother, England's a grand place, anyhow, and there's lots of money going there.'

Parnell rose up from his chair and said severely – 'Jerry O'Sullivan, do you know what you are talking about? True, that England is rich, but is money all that a man is to seek after? If the good men leave poor Ireland to make a little more money for themselves, what is to become of her? Is it not as if she was sold for money; and if you look at the real difference of wages – the wages that good sober men that can work, get here and there, a poor price she would be sold for after all.'

'I don't like that way of putting it,' said Jerry, rather testily. 'In fact I have almost made up my mind to go, and I don't think I'm selling my country at all at all, and I wish you wouldn't say such things.'

Parnell said nothing for a few moments. Then he tore the picture out of his note-book and handed it to him saying –

'Jerry, old boy, if you ever do go, keep that in your purse, and if ever you go to pay for liquor for yourself or others, just think what it means.'

When the party rose up to go they found that Katey had been crying quietly, and her eyes were red and swollen.

Jerry O'Sullivan's home was happy, and his poor, good little wife feared a change.

3

𝔄n 𝔒pening

Jerry O'Sullivan's desire to go to England was no mere transient wish. As has been told, he had had for years a strong desire to try his fortune in a country other than his own; and although the desire had since his marriage fallen into so sound a sleep that it resembled death, still it was not dead but sleeping.

Deep in the minds of most energetic persons lies some strong desire, some strong ambition, or some resolute hope, which unconsciously moulds, or, at least, influences their every act. No matter what their circumstances in life may be, or how much they may yield to those circumstances for a time, the one idea remains ever the same. This is, in fact, one of the secrets of how individual force of character comes out at times. The great idea, whatever it may be, sits enthroned in the mind, and round it gather subordinate wishes and resolves, as the feudal nobles round the King, and so goes on the chain down the whole gamut of man's nature from the taming or suppression of his wildest passions down to the commonplace routine of his daily life.

And yet we wonder at times to see, when occasion offers, with what astonishing rapidity certain individuals assert themselves, and how, when a strange circumstance arises, some new individual arises along with it, as though the man and the hour were predestined for each other.

We need not wonder if we will but think that all along the man was ready, girt in his armour, resolved in his cause, and merely awaiting, although, perhaps, he knew it not, the opportunity to manifest himself.

Whilst Jerry had been working – and working so honestly and well that he was on the high road to success – he never once abandoned in his secret heart the idea of seeking a

wider field for his exertion. Truly, Alexander has his proto-
types in every age and country; and men even try to look
ever beyond the horizon of their hopes, sighing for new
worlds when the victories of the old have been achieved.

From the receipt of Sebright's letter, Jerry had found the
old wish reviving stronger than ever. He was so prosperous
that the idea of failure in work seemed too far away to be
easily realised; and his home was so happy that domestic
trouble was absolutely beyond his comprehension.

The holy admonition – 'Ye that stand take heed lest ye
fall,' should be ever before the minds of men.

Katey saw her husband's secret wish gradually growing
into a resolve, with unutterable pain; and tried to combat
Jerry's views but hopelessly. At first he listened, and argued
the matter over fairly in all its aspects, being ever kind-
hearted and tender, and seeming to thoroughly sympathise
with her views; but as the weeks wore on, he began to take a
different tone, and without losing any of his kindness or
tenderness to express more decided opinions and intentions.
The change was so gradual that even Katey's wifely love,
and the acuteness which is the handmaiden of love, could see
no cause for change, nor could mark any time as being the
period of a definite change.

In fact, the masculine resolution was asserting itself over
the feminine, and acting and reacting in itself, but constantly in the direction of settled purpose.

With the feeling of power which a man of average mental
calibre feels over a woman of similar status amongst her own
sex, comes a fuller purpose – a more decided, definite resolve
to the man himself. Thus, Jerry, whilst arguing with his
wife, had been all the time strengthening his own resolve,
and working himself up to the belief that immediate action
was necessary to his success in life.

Wives, be careful how you argue with your husbands, for
you walk on a ridge between two precipices. If you allow a
half-formed wish to be the parent of immediate action on
your husband's part, without raising a warning voice should
you see danger that he does not, then you do him a wrong
which will surely recoil on your own head and the heads of
your children. But if, on the other hand, you persistently

combat with argument wishes which should be furthered or
opposed with the patent truths of the heart's experience,
then you will surely fail, for you will be fighting reality with
vacuity – opposing steel with air-drawn daggers of the fancy.

Katey's position was very painful. She felt that her
speaking to her husband was a duty which her wifely vow, as
much as her wifely love, called on her to fulfil; but at the
same time she felt with that subtle instinct of true love
which never errs and never lies, that she was sapping the
foundations of her husband's love and weakening the influence which she had over him. Poor Katey! her lot was a hard
one, but she felt – and she was right – that where duty
points the way, then the way must be walked whatever be
the misery of the journey, and wherever the road may lead.

Jerry's mother, too, was fretted by her son's determination. He never spoke of it to her, but she heard it from their
mutual friends, and the very fact of his being reticent on the
point caused her more pain by raising doubts as to his
motive, not only for going, but concealing his wish from her.
Jerry had a two-fold reason for his silence. Firstly, he did not
wish to give her pain, and thought that by keeping silent on
the point she would be spared at least the agony of looking
forward to his departure. In this, Jerry, like many of his
fellows, fell into the same error, which leads the hunted
ostrich to hide its head in the sand – the error which we
make when we think that shutting our eyes means shutting
out the danger which we wish to avoid. Again, Jerry wished
to avoid pain to himself.

The analysis of a sensual nature shows two evil qualities,
which, although not always expressed, are, nevertheless,
ruling powers – obstinacy and cruelty. No matter how these
qualities may be counterbalanced by other qualities as good
as these are bad, or no matter how well they are disguised,
these two evil powers have here their home. Obstinacy in its
hardest light is the adherence to a line of action begun for its
end to be gained rather than for its duty; and cruelty is
almost its logical consequence, for it is by its direct or indi-
rect means that obstacles are cleared away or points of
vantage unworthily gained. Jerry's nature was a sensual
one, although it had ever been held in check.

The power of evil has a home in every human heart. In one it is a palace vast and splendid, so splendid and vast that to the onlooker there are no dark nooks, no gloomy corners, but where all is so rich and noble that there is dignity in everything. In another it is a shooting-box only visited for motives of pleasure. In another it is an office where gold and secrecy are synonymous terms. In another it is a villa. In another a lowly hut. In Jerry it was the last; but no one is to suppose that because it was a hut, that, therefore, it was unimportant. The residents in palaces are usually to a certain extent migratory, but the inhabitants of huts are seldom absentees, and every Irishman knows that a perpetually resident peasant is better for a country than a lordly absentee.

Thus Jerry's devil, although living in a small house, was still always there, and was ever on the spot when opportunities occurred.

One change – one decided change – came which Katey regretted exceedingly, and that was in his friendship for Parnell. Hitherto the two men had been excellent friends, and Jerry's success in some little business ventures was largely due to Parnell's wise counsel. But now the two men were seldom together, and the elder one seemed to have lost all his old influence over his companion.

Parnell saw the change as well as Katey, and was deeply grieved. He, however, saw, whilst he saw the change, what danger there was in alluding to it, and so as he was one of those men who feel it almost as much a breach of duty to be silent on certain occasions as to bespeak falsely, wisely kept aloof and waited for a fitting opportunity for speaking earnestly to Jerry without the risk of offending him.

Jerry, too, knew of the change in himself, and felt a sort of hostile indignation with all who opposed openly or tacitly his determination.

This was the first manifestation of the cruelty of his nature.

His mother was broken-hearted, and in her grief, when arguing with him, unwisely gave play to her bitterness, and so hardened up one of the softest spots in his heart. She abused Sebright also, and, as some of the charges which she brought against him were manifestly absurd, Jerry took occasion to think, and to express his thoughts, that they were all absurd.

The devil works through love as well as hatred, and his blows are more deadly when we who strike and we who bear alike heed them not.

One day there came a letter from John Sebright, which influenced Jerry vitally. It was as follows:–

'Kingficher Arms, Sundy.*

'Dear Jerry – You had better come over here at wanse, there is a place to sute you in a theatre called the Stanly, where the wants a carpentre to manage for them; he must be a good man or he won't doo, and the wagis is fine, not to say exsiv, and the place esy and the people nice. you had best tri for it at wanse, and don't let the chance slip, or you will be a damd fool, and not worth gettin' another. don't let your mother or your wife keep you back, as the will tri to, for weemen isn't able to do bisnis, but men is; an' the maneger has a nefew, who is a friend o' mine an' a capatle felo, an' a hed like iren, an'mony is goin' heer lik water, an' a man with your hed wood make a fortin in no tim, which let me no at wanse til I tel the nephew, which if you give me a £1 tu give him to speek for you, it will be all rite, and send the money by return to me, care of Mrs Smith, Kingficher Arms, Welbred-street, London, and i remane
yours trooly.

'John Sebright.

'P.S. – don't sho this to your wif or mother, or the'l think i wance to mak you cum, an' av corse mi motivs is dis-intrested, as i'm wel off miself an' quit hapy.

'P.S. 2. – if you tel the weemen tel them i'm goin' to be marrid to a good woman ho is very pias an' charetable an' wel off don't forget the £1.'

Jerry was no fool, and very clearly he saw through the motive of the writer of this precious epistle, but there were passages in it which interested him deeply. Notwithstanding

---

*   Spelling and punctuation in this letter are taken from *The Shamrock*.

the mean selfishness of the man's thoughts, and the vile
English in which they were expressed, he could not shut his
eyes to certain things which they suggested, chiefly the
opening as theatrical carpenter.

Jerry had never heard of the Stanley Theatre, and even
now had not the ghost of an idea what it was like or of what
class; nevertheless, he could not help thinking that it might
be something good. London has a big name, and people who
live out of it have traditionally an idea that everything there
is great, and rich, and flourishing, and happy.

The people who live in it can tell a different story, and
point to hundreds and thousands of the poorest and most
wretched creatures that exist on the face of God's beautiful
world – the world that He has made beautiful, but that man
has defaced with sin.

Jerry was in that state in which a man finds everything
which happens exactly suiting his own views. His eyes – the
eyes of his inner self – were so full of his project that they
were incapable of seeing anything but what bore on its
advancement. He shut his eyes to dangers and defects and
difficulties, and like many another man leaped blindly into
the dark.

Sometimes to leap in the dark is the perfection of wisdom
and courage combined; but this is when the gloom which is
round us is a danger, from which we must escape at any
hazard, and not when we make an artificial night by wilfully
shutting our eyes upon the glory of the sun.

Jerry wrote to Sebright, enclosing a Post-office order for
one pound and telling him to lose no time about seeing after
the situation for him.

He said not a word about what he had done, even to poor
little Katey, who saw with the eyes of her love that he was
keeping something back from her.

It was the first secret of their married life, and the bright
eyes were dim from silent weeping as the little wife rose the
morning after the letter to London was despatched.

Several days elapsed before Jerry got any reply from
London; and the interval was an unhappy time for both him
and his wife. Katey's grief grew heavier and heavier to her
since she had no one to tell it to; and Jerry felt that there

was a shadow between them. He recked not that it was the shadow of his own selfish desire – the spectre of the future – that stood between them.

Katey's lot was hard. The sweetest blessing of marriage is that it halves our sorrows and doubles our joys; and so far as her present life went Katey was a widow in this respect – but without the sweet consolation that married trust had never died.

Jerry's anxiety made the home trouble light. He had, like most men to whom the world behind the curtain is as unknown as were the mysteries of Isis to a Neophyte, a strange longing to share in the unknown life of the dramatic world. Moth-like he had buzzed around the footlights when a boy, and had never lost the slight romantic feeling which such buzzing ever inspires. Once or twice his professional work had brought him within the magic precincts where the stage-manager is king, and there the weirdness of the place, with its myriad cords and chains, and traps, and scenes, and flies, had more than ever enchanted him.

The chance now offered of employment was indeed a temptation. If he should be able to adopt the new life he would have an opportunity of combining his romantic taste and his trade experience, and would be moreover in that wider field for exertion to which he had long looked forward.

And so he waited with what patience he could, and shut his eyes as close as possible to the growing miseries of his home.

At last a letter came from Sebright, telling him that he had got the place, and one also from the manager, stating that he would have to be at work in a fortnight's time, and stating the salary, which was very liberal.

Face to face with the situation, Jerry found that the sooner he told his wife the better. He took the day to think over his plans, and when he went home in the evening he went prepared to tell her.

There was about him a tenderness unusual of late – a tenderness which reminded Katey of the first days of their married life and of the time when her first child was born; and so the little woman's heart was touched, and woman-like she could not fear, nor even see troubles in the light of her

husband's smile. Jerry himself felt the change in her manner, and his tenderness grew. He took her on his knees, as in
their old courting days, and a few sweet whispered words
brought the colour to her cheek, and the old light into her
eyes. Then it was that Jerry felt how hard was the news
which he had to tell, and he half repented of his resolution.
He thought of the happy home which he was breaking up,
and of the anguish of the little wife and mother who was to
be taken away from all her friends and relatives to begin the
world anew amongst strangers. But the time was come when
he must speak, for to delay would be cruel, and so he began
with a huskiness in his throat which was not usual to him.

'Katey, dear, I've some news for you.'

Katey's arms tightened round his neck.

'Oh, and good news too, Jerry, I know by your tenderness
to me to-night. Jerry dear, have you given up the wild idea?'

Jerry did not expect this, and his voice became a little
harder as he replied –

'No, I have not given up the wild idea, as you call it. It is
about it that I want to speak.'

Katey felt the shadow pass between them again, and in
spite of all she could do her eyes filled with tears. She did not
wish to hurt Jerry, however, and turned away her head. But,
man-like, he would know all that was going on in the mind of
his companion, and, taking her face between his strong
hands, he turned it up to the light. As he did so, he saw the
tears and could not help feeling annoyed, for he knew that as
yet in the conversation he had said nothing to warrant the
change from sunshine to rain. So he spoke not unkindly –

'Cryin' already. Ah, Katey, what do you mean?'

'Nothin', Jerry, nothin', my dear, only I couldn't help it.
I'm not very strong yet.' She said this with a tender, half shy
glance down at the cradle, which she was rocking with her
foot, that would have turned the heart of a savage.

Jerry could not help feeling moved, and clasped her still
more tenderly in his strong arms, and his voice softened –

'Sure, Katey, it's breakin' my heart I am all day knowin'
how you would take the news. Cry away, darlin', it'll do you
good, and mayhap the news will make you cry.'

'No, no, Jerry, only talk to me like that, and I'll never cry

– never – never – never.' The little woman's voice went up in a sweet, half playful crescendo as she reiterated the last words, and shook aside her tears.

'Then, Katey, I'll tell you. I have got an offer to go to England' – Katey's face fell – 'to London – to become head carpenter in a theatre, an' I've written to say I'll take it.'

Woman's nature, when compared with man's, resembles more the hare than his does, and her moral eye, like the hare's eye, is set far back for seeing the past clearly, whilst it accepts the future blindly. She accepts facts more easily than resolves; and when once a thing has been accomplished, and any final or decisive step taken, the major part of her anxiety is over. Accordingly Katey heard her husband's resolve with an equanimity which took him by surprise. She did not cry, although her heart felt to herself to sink into her very boots, but simply drew his head on her bosom and stroked his hair, saying fervently –

'God grant, Jerry, acushla,* that it may be for the best. May all the saints pray for us both.'

'Amen,' said Jerry, and then both remained silent for a time.

Soon the woman's curiosity spoke, and her imagination began to work; and in the pleasure of expectation of change – always specially dear to women – she lost sight for a time of her present trouble. She began to question Jerry about the new engagement, and, having once began, poured forth such a tide of questions that he had no time to answer them, even had he known himself all she wanted. He did as well as he could, however; and now that the worst of the news was over, her hopeful nature took the brightest view possible of the case, and she seemed, by comparison with her mood of the last few days, quite happy.

Jerry did not tell her that night of the time of leaving, but let her sleep with what happiness she could, for he knew that the morrow, when she had learned the necessary suddenness of their departure, would be a sad one for her.

In the morning he told her just before going to his work, for he put off the evil moment, half that she might be able to

---

*   acushla – (Irish) darling or sweetheart.

have her cry in quietness – he knew that she would cry – and half with a man's selfish wish to avoid an unpleasant scene.

Katey bore up till he was gone, and then the tide of her grief and sorrow burst forth unchecked, and she cried so pitifully that her little ones began to cry from childish sympathy. She took them in her arms and knelt down with them and rocked herself and them to and fro, and moaned –

'Oh, woe the day, oh, woe the day.'

4

The New Life

J erry O'Sullivan well knew the difference between the dispositions of his wife and his mother; and it was not without a shrinking of spirit that he approached the dwelling of the latter that evening to impart the unwelcome news.

His fears were not without foundation, for when he began to tell his news the old lady who had hitherto been full of love and affection broke out into a desperate fit of crying, a very unusual thing with her, mingling her tears with reproaches such as Jerry had never before heard from her lips.

'And you, my son,' she said, 'are about to leave your home, and your country, and your mother, and to go amongst strangers. Oh, woe the day, oh, woe the day, that my child ever wants to leave the ground where his poor dead father lies sleeping. Oh, Jerry, Jerry, was it for this that I watched over your youth, and toiled and slaved for you, early and late, that when I saw you grow into a strong, steady, honest man, with a sweet wife and a happy home, I should see you leave me for ever.'

Jerry interrupted. 'Not for ever, mother.'

'Ay, ay, for ever. *Wirrasthrue, wirrasthrue.** Sure, don't I know I'll never see your face again. You're goin', Jerry, among strangers an' their ways are not our ways, and amongst them you'll forget the lessons of your home. You're goin' to a city where the devil lives, if he lives any one place in the world; and I must sit at home here and doubt, and sigh, and weep, and weep, till I die.'

'Mother, dear, don't take on like this. Why should you doubt, and sigh, and weep at all, at all? I amn't goin' to do

---

*   wirrasthru – (Irish) an exclamation of sorrow or lament.

anything wrong. I'm goin' to work harder than ever, an' I think, mother – I do think that it's not fair to me to think that I'm goin' to go to the devil, just because I leave one town to live in another.'

But reason and consolation were alike thrown away on Mrs O'Sullivan. The spice of obstinacy in her nature, and which Jerry had inherited from her, made her stick to her point; and so after many efforts Jerry came away leaving her bowed down with sorrow. He was himself somewhat indignant – and with fair enough reason – that all his relatives should take it for granted that he was going to change an honest hardworking life for an idle dissolute one.

He did not like to go home at once, for he somehow felt afraid of meeting a reproachful look on Katey's face. This fear was a proof that he knew in his secret heart that he was doing wrong, for in all their married life Katey had never once given him cause for such a thought; it was in his own conscience that the reproach arose; and the look was on the face of his angel.

Accordingly, he made a detour and called at the house of Mr Muldoon. The great man was within and received him heartily.

'Why, O'Sullivan,' said he, 'this is quite unexpected. Sit down, man, and make yourself comfortable.'

Jerry sat down, but was anything but comfortable. Whilst he was on the way to his home, he had felt a desire to stay away, but now that he was settled down he longed to be at home. Katey's face, pale with her recent sickness, and paler still from her recent grief, seemed to look at him, and he thought and felt how her poor heart must be beating as she waited and waited for his return, counting the minutes, and finding in each moment's extra delay new causes for dread. At last he could stand it no longer and jumped up, saying to his host:

'I can't stay. I have not been at home yet, and Katey will be expecting me.'

Muldoon laughed.

'There's a man with three children! Sure, a wife in her honeymoon wouldn't look for you like that.'

'Katey would, and does. No, indeed, I can't stay. I just

came to tell you that I have got an engagement in the Stanley Theatre, in London, as carpenter, and I am going in less than a fortnight.'

Mr Muldoon whistled.

'This is sudden,' he said.

'Ay,' said Jerry, but said no more.

'You must come and spend an evening with me before you go, and your mother will come and Marg–, Miss M'Anaspie; and we'll get the boys and girls and have great fun.'

'Agree,' said Jerry, and took his leave.

When he got home Katey flew to the door to meet him, and clung to him and kissed him, and he wondered how he could be such a fool as to stop away for fear of any reproach from her. He told her of his visit to his mother and Mr Muldoon, and of the invitation of the latter, which she agreed should be accepted.

The next week was such a busy one that neither Jerry nor Katey had much time for repining, and even Mrs O'Sullivan found some consolation in her exertions and the liberal preparations which she was making for her son's departure. At first there was some question as to the advisability of Katey and the children going at once, as some of the family thought that it would be better if Jerry went alone and Katey waited to follow when all was comfortably settled for her. Katey herself had, however, put a stop at once to the discussion.

'I don't want comfort,' she said, 'and I amn't afraid to rough it since we are to go; but I want to be with Jerry.'

Her mother-in-law backed her up in this view, and so the matter was arranged.

Mr Muldoon's entertainment was a great affair. No expense had been spared on the host's part, and no trouble on the part of his servant; and the consequence was an amount of splendour which dazzled all beholders.

The entertainment was given in the drawingroom over the shop, a room seldom entered save by the servant, who periodically dusted it. The covers had been taken off the chairs which now showed their red cushions in all their splendour. The yellow gauze had been removed from the mirror, the picture frames, and the gaselier, which no longer

presented its habitual appearance – that of an immense jelly
bag, through which yokes of egg have passed. The eating and
drinking was on a scale of magnificence. Not only had the
warehouse been ransacked for its delicacies, but good things
of, so to speak, an alien description had been provided, and
so far as the inner-man was concerned nothing was wanting.
The company was the same as that at the christening party,
with the addition of a couple of hard dry old men, of whom
Mr Muldoon thought much, and to whom he paid decided
deference.

When all the company had assembled, which was about
seven o'clock, Mr Muldoon ordered supper, and all went
vigorously to work. Hitherto there had been a little stiffness.
Price and Carey had been somewhat awed by Mr Muldoon's
magnificence, and their sweethearts, seeing this, had followed their lead, and remained in seemingly bashful silence.
Jerry and Katey, and Mrs O'Sullivan, and Parnell, were too
heavy-hearted for mirth, and so the only members of the
party who were lively, were the host and Miss M'Anaspie.

The latter was anything but sorrowful, and truly with
good cause. She saw with the instinct of her sex that she had
made a conquest in the rich old bachelor, and already tasted
possession of all the splendour which surrounded her. She
was even now, whilst she pretended to admire, planning
changes in the room and its furniture. The chairs would not
be arranged as at present, the pictures were too gloomy, and
would have to be replaced by others of brighter hue – in fact,
altogether much additional splendour would have to be
imported, so that all her friends and visitors would be driven
to the wildest envy without giving them a chance of escape.

When the supper was done, Mr Muldoon stood up and
made a speech reverting to Jerry's departure, and wishing
him success, and also managing to bring in a neat compli-
ment to Miss M'Anaspie's good looks, which caused that
bashful young female to hide her face in her pockethandker-
chief and to giggle for some minutes. Before he sat down he
said, and said it pointedly –

'The last meeting of a festive description at which we all
assisted was, I think, somewhat spoiled by various discussions. Now, I hope that to-night we will have no such

discussions. I wish that our friends, Jerry and Katey, may have an evening all jolly and merry.'

'Hear, hear,' said the old men, simultaneously.

Parnell felt that all this was levelled at him, and found his hands tied. There was no discussion of any kind, and as nothing more than casual remarks were made, the party soon took a tone so gloomy that even the lively Margaret found her spirits below zero. All this tended to irritate Mr Muldoon. A man of his temperament gets dogmatic in proportion to his irritation, and consequently he soon was laying down the law on every imaginable point.

This still more increased the gloom till all was so deadly that Katey could bear it no longer, and left earlier than she had intended. The rest were not slow to follow her example, and Mr Muldoon was so enraged at the miserable failure of his merry party that he would hardly say good night.

The days drew on towards their departure, and all were so busy that there was no time for thought – perhaps just as well for those of them that had hearts to feel.

At last the day arrived, and their friends assembled at the North-wall to see them off, for they were going by sea on account of their luggage, which was quite disproportionate to their rank in life. The anguish of parting was very great, and the tears shed many. But partings must ever be, and this one was like all that have gone before and all that are to follow after. So great was the grief of all that Jerry for a time repented of his determination.

And so Jerry O'Sullivan and his wife and children left home and fortune to seek greater fortune in a strange place.

The voyage lasted three days. For the first twenty-four hours Katey was too sick to think, and the poor children suffered dreadfully; and it was not till the black bare rocks of the Land's End came into view that the poor little woman was able to look about her. Even the first glimpse of her future country was not reassuring, for it looked very black and cheerless and inhospitable indeed.

However, by the time Falmouth, with its houses clustered up the hill, and its quaint, quiet, old-world look still upon it, came in sight, her spirits rose. From thence the journey was enjoyed by all, for the weather was fine and the sea like glass. The south coast of England is full of charming scenery, which one sees much of in passing from port to port, and it was no wonder that Jerry and his wife felt somewhat elated at being amongst such wealth and security as the disposition of things there presupposed. Plymouth, the queen of ports, with its wealth of naval strength and its picturesque batteries on Mound Edgecombe, Drake Island, and the Hoe; and Portsmouth, guarded by iron-clad towers out in the very sea, miles of continuous batteries and innumerable war-ships, made a deep impression, and somehow Katey felt that Jerry was a cleverer man than she had given him credit for being.

It is the nature of the greater to absorb the lesser. We see the beauty of the rose in full luxuriance in the summer sunlight; it is only when we reach the core that we find the canker worm.

At last the Thames was reached, and the O'Sullivans were fairly awed by the strength of the defences. All up the river, which took them the best part of a day to ascend, the banks were studded with forts on either side. Little low-lying forts, all fronted with iron, dangerous places, very hard to hit from any distance away, but able to contain the best and biggest guns made in the world; the black iron-cased ports, in rows seemingly level with the water's edge, looked like the iron doors of the vaults in a cemetery, a fact which, in the eyes of the onlookers, added not a little to the grim terror of their appearance. The wonder culminated at Tilbury, for here two immense forts defended the narrowest part of the river, and made the idea of any hostile force passing up it a complete impossibility.

London was reached at last. Busy, bustling, rushing, hurrying London, compared with which all other cities seem as the castle of the sleeping princess in the fairy tale; and Jerry and his wife, on landing from the steamer, albeit they came from a city where Progress speaks with no puny voice and works with no lazy hand, felt bewildered.

At the best of times and places a landing-stage is no flower garden, especially to the incomer; but the London landing-stages, with their great steam-cranes and palatial warehouses, and ships lying seven or eight deep out into the river, are wonders in themselves. It was only by patience, and care, and asking many questions that Jerry was able to bring his family into the wholly terrestrial world.

Through much bustling, scrambling, and exertion, they found their way into the street where the theatre was situated, for as they knew nothing about the place Jerry thought it best to get as near to his work as he could. He had high resolves, and intended to work harder even in the new life than in the old.

The neighbourhood was exceedingly poor, and an amount of misery and squalor prevailed which showed Katey in as many moments as the other had taken hours that all was not gold which glittered within the strip of silver sea which her sons call Britain's bulwarks, but that the greatness, and wealth, and strength, have their counterfoils in crime, and poverty, and disease.

More than an hour was spent in looking for lodgings, and Katey's heart was sick and sore. There was some vital objection to every place. One was too dear, another was too dirty, a third was too small, and so on.

All things have an end, even looking for lodgings, and towards nightfall they lighted on a place, which, although not exactly what they required, was still the nearest approach to it that they had yet come across. It was over a green-grocer's shop, and promised to be fairly comfortable. Katey, somehow, felt that the mere show of green stuff gave it a little of the idea of home – just enough, she found out afterwards, to make her home sickness, which had worn somewhat away during the last day or two, come back again.

However, she had no time for brooding over sorrows, real or sentimental. The children were dead tired and crying with sleep, and so when a fire was lit, and the basket of provisions opened, they were tucked into their bed and fell asleep in a moment.

Whilst Katey was thus attending to her household duties, Jerry was exercising his professional skill in making the room comfortable, knocking up nails here and there, and generally improving the disposition of affairs. Both had finished about the same time, and then Katey made the tea, and the husband and wife sat down to chat, she sitting on his knee as all loving little wives love to sit.

Jerry now felt face to face with the realities of his new life, and the prospect was not all cheering. He missed the comforts of home, and felt, in spite of his strong wilful self-belief which deadens a mind like his to many outward miseries, that he was but an atom in the midst of the world around him – a grain of sand in that great desert which men call London. Katey was more cheerful, for a wife carries with her husband and children her true home which rests as securely in her heart as a snail's-house on his back. Katey slept that night, for she was tired out, but Jerry could not sleep.

In the morning he was stirring by daylight, and after lighting the fire, for Katey was so worn out that she still slept, went out to look about the neighbourhood. It was still so early that but few people were up. He found his way to the theatre, whose external appearance filled him with consternation. The outside of a small theatre is at the best of times unpromising, and this one looked, in the cool morning air, squalid in the extreme.

Jerry wandered round it curiously trying to get every possible view. As it went back into a large block of buildings, this was no sort of easy task; and so by the time the survey was completed he was quite ready for his breakfast.

Katey was up and as bright as a bee. The children had recovered their good temper in their sleep, and everything was infinitely more cheerful than had seemed possible for it ever to be the night before.

Katey came up to her husband as he entered the room and put her arms round his neck and kissed him several times very, very fondly.

'God bless our future life, Jerry, dear,' she said, 'I hope it will always be as happy as this. If I can do it be sure your home will always be a cheerful and happy one.'

He kissed her in return, feeling more deeply than he cared to say, for there was a rising lump in his throat.

The morning passed in settling things straight, and in the afternoon Jerry went down to the theatre again. The place looked more lively than before, although in reality still very dismal. There were a few of those nondescript, ill-clad loungers that are only seen in the precincts of theatres, hanging round the door – those seedy specimens of humanity who are the camp-followers of the histrionic army.

When Jerry asked one of them where he would find the manager, he winked at his companions, rubbed his lips, and said, with obsequious alacrity –

'This way, sir. Come with me and I'll show you the way.'

Jerry followed him through several dark passages filled with innumerable boxes of all sizes – old woodwork and portions of scenic ornamentation half covered with tarnished gilding, till they reached a door, to which the guide pointed, saying –

'It's a very dry day, your honour.'

'Very dry,' said Jerry.

'A drop would not be bad, sir.'

Jerry's appearance was so good that the man called him sir, not all for the purpose of flattering his small vanity.

Jerry gave him twopence, and knocked at the door.

He was told to come in, and on doing so found the manager who was just going out, and who, being in a hurry, told him to come to him next morning to talk over his duties, and in the meantime to see the stage-manager, Mr Griffin, who would show him over the place, so that he might get accustomed to it.

Jerry managed to find his way to the stage, which was lit by a great line of gas-jets on the top of a vertical pipe, like a hayrake, stuck at the back of the orchestra. A dress rehearsal was going on, and Jerry stood in the wing to watch. The play was a version of Faust, and the dresses were the same as those used in Gounod's opera. Presently, Mr Griffin noticed the strange face, and came over to the wing. Jerry told him his name, and was at once welcomed as a member of the staff. He was introduced to several people on the stage with whom he was likely to come in contact. Amongst the actors was a tall individual who was performing the part of 'Mephistopheles,' who came over to Jerry and introduced himself, saying that he knew John Sebright. Jerry was glad to see anyone who had the tie of a mutual friend amongst so many strange faces, and, although he did not like the appearance of his new friend, spoke to him heartily.

Whenever he had an opportunity during the course of the rehearsal he came over to Jerry and resumed their chat. Presently he came over and said –

'I am not on in this scene. Come and have a glass of beer with me.'

'With pleasure,' said Jerry, for he was hot and thirsty, and the twain adjourned to a little tavern across the street, Mons, the new friend, calling into his dressing room to put on his Ulster coat, so that his stage dress would not be observed.

When they entered the tavern the bar-keeper was busy settling his glasses, and had his back turned to them. Mons took off his Ulster and sat down, there being no one but themselves present except a drunken shoemaker, whom Mons knew, and a beggarman who followed them in.

When the bar-keeper turned round Jerry met the most repulsive face he had ever seen – a face so drawn and twisted, with nose and lips so eaten away with some strange canker, that it resembled more the ghastly front of a skull than the face of a living man. Jerry was shocked, but in the meantime Mons called for the beer, which was brought and soon drunk.

Mons then said –

'Grinnell, this is our new carpenter.'

'Glad to see you, sir. Welcome to London. I understand you're Irish. You beat us there in one thing, at all events.'

'What is that?' said Jerry.

'Your whisky. We can get none like it; but I tell you what, I'll give you some liquor you never tasted, I'll be bound. And as you're a stranger I'll make it a present to you.'

'No, no,' said Jerry.

'Take it,' whispered Mons. 'He'll be offended if you don't.'

Grinnell produced a bottle of labelled 'Gift' from the shelf, and poured out two half tumblers full and handed one to each.

'That's what I give for my hansel,' said Grinnell. 'What do you think of it?'

'Capital,' said Jerry, after tasting it. 'What is it called. I see 'Gift' on the bottle?'

WELCOME TO LONDON

'No, that's not its name. I put that on it to show my cus-
tomers that when I give it I mean civility and not commerce.
It's a decoction I make myself.'

Just then a boy ran across from the theatre and said –

'Mr Mons, you're wanted. Your scene is on.'

Mons tried to put his hand into his pocket, but could not
as his tights had no pockets. He said to Jerry as he went out –

'I've got no money with me. Will you pay for the beer and
I'll give it you when you come back to the theatre.'

'All right,' said Jerry, and he took out his purse.

As he opened it he saw Parnell's picture, and then it
struck him that his new life was beginning but badly,
drinking in the middle of the day.

He paid the money and went quickly out of the public
house without looking behind him.

5

How the New Life began

When Jerry got back to the theatre the place did not somehow look the same; there was too much tarnished gilding, he thought, and too little reality. Although the place seemed very old and dirty – so old and so dirty that after looking about him for a little time he felt that there was room and opportunity for all his skill and energy – there was something so cheering in this prospect of hard work that he forgave the dirt and the age, and longed to get into active service.

The rehearsal did not take much longer, and then the various actors and employés dispersed. Mons came over to Jerry and asked him to come to his dressing-room for a moment. Jerry was anxious to get home, and said so.

'You need not fear,' said Mons. 'I shan't detain you a minute. I only want to give you what you paid for me.'

'Nonsense, man,' said Jerry, who felt almost insulted, for, like all Irishmen, he had one virtue which too often leans to vice's side – generosity, and considered that hospitality was involved in the question of 'who pays?'

Of all the silly ideas that ever grew in the minds of a people, feeding on their native generosity of disposition, this idea is the most silly. Let any man but think honestly how honour or hospitality can be involved in the mere payment of a few pence, and then ask himself the question in his heart of what difference there is to him between the nobler virtues of his soul and the pride of superabundant coinage. Jerry O'Sullivan was no fool, and often reasoned with himself on the subject; but still the prejudice of habit was too strong within him to be easily overcome, and so he felt hurt in spite of his reasons. Mons answered him suavely –

'No nonsense at all. I borrowed a small sum of money off

you, which you kindly lent me. I now wish to repay you.'

'Sure there isn't need of repayment because I paid for a glass of beer.'

'But a debt is a debt, large or small, and I don't want to remain due to any man.'

Jerry thought for a moment or two. The justness of the statement struck him so forcibly that he felt that any further talk would be unfair to his friend; so answered simply – 'Fair enough,' and took the money proffered, thinking to himself what a good-hearted, honest fellow his new friend was.

It was well nigh dark when Jerry got home. He found Katey up to her eyes in work; for between settling the rooms and unpacking, and looking after the children and the supper, she had quite enough to do. She had given the rooms a thorough cleaning – a thing very much required – and as they had not quite recovered from the effects; were not so comfortable as they might have been. The floors still presented that patchy appearance which newly-washed woodwork always assumes; and even the bright fire was not able to quite overcome the idea of damp thus suggested.

Nevertheless, the change even to unfinished cleanliness was pleasant after the unutterable grime of the theatre; and Jerry felt how pleasant was the idea of home, albeit he regretted in the core of his heart that his real home – the place where he was born and bred – was far away.

Katey bustled about; and soon the supper was ready, and in its consumption things began to assume a pleasanter aspect. All were tired and went to bed early.

In the morning Jerry was up early and round the neighbourhood looking about him. Theatrical life, save on occasions, begins late, even for the subordinates, and Jerry's services were not required till an hour which, when compared with his habitual hour for going to work, seemed to him to be closer to evening than morning. At the time appointed he was waiting to see the manager, who did not appear, however, till more than an hour after his engagement. Jerry waited with impatience for his coming. To a man habitually as well as naturally active in occupation, nothing is so tiresome as that of waiting: it is only the drones in the hive of life that enjoy idleness in the midst of others' work.

It is the misery of all those whose work is connected with the arts that there is a spice of uncertainty in everything. It would seem as if Providence had decreed that those who soar above the level of commonplace humanity should bear with them some counterbalancing weakness to show them that they are but of the level after all. The ancients showed this idea by an allegory in the story of him who, with wings of wax, thinking himself no longer a mortal, but a god, flew close to the sun till the waxen pinions melted, and he fell prone.

Jerry was in no good humour at the end of his long wait, and more than once the idea occurred to him that a theatre was a very dry place. Fortunately, however, he was afraid to leave his post, or else Mr Grinnell might have benefitted by his thirst.

When the manager, Mr Meredith, came in he spoke to Jerry in an off-hand way, telling him what his duties would be, and what his salary; that he should be always up to time; that he should keep his subordinates in good order, and so forth; and ended by sending him off to Mr Griffin to find out the details of his work.

Mr Griffin was available, for the rehearsal of the day was only that of a stock piece, whose management he could trust to the hands of the prompter. He went right over the stage with Jerry, showing him the various appliances and their manner of use. Jerry's practised mind at once took in what was required in each case, and he saw his way to many improvements, to execute which his hands itched. The new style of work was not a little confusing, however, and the names of the different things got so mixed up that when he was asleep that night Jerry kept dreaming of slots, and flies, and wings, and flats, and vampire traps, and grooves, and PS (prompt side), and OP (opposite prompt side), all which got jumbled together and puzzled him not a little. He was not required at the theatre in the night time for a couple of days, and so spent the evenings at home.

At last he got regularly to work, and began his task of re-organisation, commencing by trying a general cleaning up. After half-an-hour's work he was astonished. He could not have believed that any place could be so dirty, or that such a

pile of dust and rubbish of every kind could have been accu-
mulated into the space from which the pile before him had
been removed. In the cleaning process he had got so dry that
he found it necessary to have a drink, and accordingly he
went to a corner of the cellar, where there was a tap, to get
some water. As he was about to drink, Mons, who had followed him, spoke –

'You don't mean to say you're drinking water at this time
of day?'

'Bedad I am. I've the thirst of the lost upon me,' and Jerry
raised his hands, of which he had made a bowl, to his lips.
Mons gave him a shove, which spilled the water.

'Don't be an ass, man,' he said. 'Have a glass of beer, or
try Barclay and Perkins.'

'What is Barclay and Perkins?'

'Entire.'

'Entire! what do you mean?'

'I mean, my dear O'Sullivan, that you are green as your
Emerald Island. Barclay and Perkins are two great philan-
thropists who aid suffering humanity by brewing a delicious
liquid called "Entire".'

'Oh, I see, they're the London Guinness.'

Mons laughed satirically. 'Exactly,' he said. He could not
fancy any one judging of anything except by a London
standard of comparison. In the meantime Jerry was getting
more thirsty than ever, and, on Mons renewing his
invitation, he went with him to Grinnell's, to see, as the
latter suggested, 'whether Ireland was equal to England in
brewing or not.'

As they were leaving the theatre Mons stopped and said –

'Hold on a moment, wait here – or stay, wait for me over
there. I want to go up to my dressing-room to get some
money.'

Jerry accordingly went across alone to the public-house.

As he opened the door his ears were greeted by sounds of
strife – curses both loud and deep, falling furniture and
breaking glass, and the scuffling and trampling of angry feet;
added to these was the ceaseless yelping of a dog.

Jerry pushed open the door hastily and entered the house.
The sight which met his eyes was not a pleasant one to a

peaceably-disposed man. Two men were struggling in the
centre of the room with all the intensity and ferocity of wild
beasts. They were not fighting 'fair,' in the ordinary accep-
tance of the term, but were clutching wildly at each other's
throats and hair, and were trying to scratch as much as to
hit. The strife evidently sprung from no desire of mastery,
but was the outcome of hatred, deadly, so far as it went.
Close by them a small table overturned, and a scattered pack
of cards spoke volumes as to the origin of the hatred. A
wretched-looking dog, whose foot had been trodden on in the
scuffle, limped under the bar, yelping. The only element of
calmness in the room was supplied in the person of Grinnell,
who, conspicuous in his white shirt sleeves, with large cuffs
and gorgeous links, leaned over his bar, complacently, resting his head on his hands and biting the tops of his fingers in
quiet enjoyment of the scene. He knew from experience that
a little *émeute** of this kind was in no wise to be discouraged,
for it always ended in 'drinks all round,' an ending of which
he, as a professional man, highly approved.

Jerry could not bear fighting. He had in himself, somewhere hidden below the outer crust of his nature, a spark of
warlike fire which his consciousness told him should not be
fanned into flame, and so, whilst his head remained clear
and his reason worked, he dreaded that which he felt in his
heart was dangerous. He was, however, an energetic man;
and it is not natural to the energetic to stand by inactive
whilst strife is being carried on. Accordingly, he rushed over
to separate the combatants.

The part of peacemaker is a noble one, and one which no
man worthy of the name should shrink from on account of its
unpleasantnesses, difficulties, or dangers; but it has its own
trials. The natural impulse of two animals, human or other-
wise, when interrupted in combat is to both turn on the
aggressor; and the experience of any man will tell him how
marked is this characteristic in the human animal. Jerry
knew this as well as most men, for, being a quiet and temperate man the burden of peacemaking fell on his shoulders
more often than on those of most of his fellows.

---

* émeute – (French) a popular rising, disturbance, or uproar.

He was not prepared, however, for the storm which fell upon him in this case. One of the combatants caught him by the hair, at which he dragged so savagely that, half to be free from the exquisite pain which it caused him, and half to end the struggle quickly, Jerry was obliged to clutch him by the throat. Having so caught him, Jerry was comparatively safe so far as this foe was concerned, for with his powerful thumb upon his throat and able to hold him at arm's length, the struggle was a matter of moments. He was not sorry for this, for he saw that his opponent was none other than John Sebright, who, however, did not seem to recognise him.

But in the meantime the second gambler was quite free and able to work out his purpose unchecked. What that purpose was Jerry had reason to remember for many a long day, for the man, who was a stoutly-built fellow enough, snatched up a chair, and, holding it by the leg in both hands, struck him over the head with it.

Jerry fell quite senseless just in time to be seen by Mons as he entered the door.

The sight of a man lying on the floor seemingly dead, save that he was bleeding copiously, called both the combatants to themselves, and instinctively they stopped and looked at him and at each other. Mons ran over and joined the group; and Grinnell, seeing that matters had gone a little too far, and fearing that his house would get a bad name, hurried out from behind his bar cursing and swearing and making a great fuss.

His first care was business. He was afraid of losing the custom of Jerry's victor by giving him offence, and equally afraid of getting into trouble if he did not take some active step against him; accordingly, he took a medium course, and coming close to him whispered:

'You had better cut, in case of a row.'

The man nodded, and taking up his coat and hat hurried out of the place.

Grinnell proceeded to act the part of the good Samaritan to Jerry, with, however, the difference that he forced the wine into his mouth instead of his cut. It takes a great deal to knock the senses out of a man for long, and Jerry's temperate life and healthy physique stood him in good stead. In

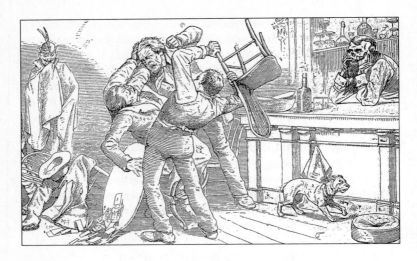

THE PLEASURES OF GAMBLING

a couple of minutes he opened his eyes, and seeing a lot of strange faces round him started into a sitting posture. The effort made his head throb, and he put his hand to it. Then he felt something strange and clammy, and looking at his hand to see what it was saw it covered with blood. This gave him a shock, which, although it made him feel sick, still further aroused him, and he stood up. He was a little weak and his head was swimming, so that he clutched at the stretched hands round him to steady himself.

By-and-bye he got better, and measures were taken to stop the bleeding of the cut in his head. He did not like the dressing of the rough unskilled hands, and went off to a neighbouring apothecary to have the wound properly attended to. Sebright had vanished from the house at an early stage of the proceedings.

All this took some time, so that when Jerry got home it was past his appointed hour, and the dinner was nearly spoiled in spite of poor Katey's efforts. In order to prevent Katey from seeing the wound, he pretended to be in a hurry to get back to his work and kept on his cap. Katey noticed that he was looking pale, and cautioned him against working too hard and going into places that were not healthy. Jerry smiled, kissed her, and went back to his work.

He was not able to do much, however, for after the rest he began to feel the real effects of the blow. He tried to work as before, but could not, and at one time got so faint that one of his men went out for some brandy, which freshened him up a bit, so that he tried to work again. Again he failed, and this time almost fainted, and again the brandy-and-water cure was resorted to. Jerry was a temperate man, and the liquor thus taken at an unusual time began to have effect on him. This made him angry, for he felt it, and having, as is known, a strong spice of obstinacy in his nature, determined not to give in to it. Therefore, instead of lying down, as Mr Griffin, who was present, wanted him to do, he insisted in going about and talking to every one, and generally laying for himself the foundation of a bad name and much distrust, for men never can have the same confidence in a man when they have once seen him off his head as they had when his wits were intact. Mons took advantage of his condition to induce him to pay Grinnell another visit, for the purpose, he said, of showing the poor man that he bore him no malice for the row that had occurred in his house. Jerry was in that state when a man thinks that to say 'yes' to everything is meritorious, and, having shaken Mons' hand several times in succession, they both adjourned over the way, followed by a little train of the hangers-on, who scented a 'free liquor' for themselves out of all this ultra-friendliness.

In the public-house they found Sebright and his sometime enemy engaged in a game of cards. They had both returned on learning that Jerry was all right, and had made up their quarrel.

When Sebright saw Jerry he rose up quickly and ran over, addressing him with much effusion.

'Why, Jerry, old man, I don't know how to look you in the face. To think that I didn't know you, and that the first time we met after so long I would be draggin' at your hair, and you clutchin' my throat. How are you? I was waitin' here hopin' to see you, and that's how the row began. Me and Popham was playin' a game while we was waitin', an' somehow we fell out, an' – but I hope you don't mind?'

Jerry was in a large-hearted mood, and answered with some thickness of speech – 'All – righ – ole – fella' – that horrid assurance of acquiescence which is the shibboleth of the drunkard. He then forgave Popham also, who made a shambling kind of excuse for his striking him.

At this stage Grinnell proposed 'glasses round,' in which proposition he was warmly supported by all those present, Jerry offering to pay the expense.

It was late that night when Jerry got home. He was left at the door of his lodgings by Mons and Sebright, and managed to stagger upstairs.

Katey, who had been sitting alone all evening in growing anxiety for his unexplained absence, heard the unusual sound he made in ascending. She knew the step that was her husband's, and yet not his, and her heart stood still in deadly fear. She was afraid to go to the door lest she should see something to horrify her, and so sat still.

The door opened and Jerry staggered in, with hair tossed, clothes all awry, and, worst pain of all to Katey's loving heart, with the bright eyes opaque, the erect form collapsing, and the firm mouth relaxed with the drunkard's feeble maundering gape.

Katey said no word but fell on her knees, lifting her hands as she lifted her soul towards heaven for forgiveness for her poor husband.

It was the first time Jerry had ever been drunk, and it struck his poor wife a blow as cruel as the stroke of death.

'Oh, Jerry, Jerry,' she moaned in her heart, 'my love, my husband, better we had stayed at home than this – oh, God, than *this*.'

6

𝔄 𝔖ummons

The next morning was a bitter one. Katey had been crying all night, whilst Jerry lay in his drunken sleep, tears which even her prayers could not stop. To her this fall of Jerry's was but the beginning of the end, and she had wept as one who looks into the future, and sees there the moving shadow of hopeless misery, blighting and darkening everything. Towards morning her tears had stopped, partly from exhaustion, and partly because she had made a noble effort to overcome her feelings, in order that Jerry might see hope, and not despair, in her face, when he awoke.

Now, as the pale cold light was stealing in through the little window, all seemed cheerless indeed.

There is something dreadfully severe in the test of early morning light. Under it everything assumes its most real aspect; there is no use trying to hide or conceal anything from it, for out the truth will surely come. Those who fear it have no option but to shut it out altogether, and wait in darkness or artificial light, till a sun that has shone on more iniquity and untruth can look on them and their deeds, without crying shame to all the world.

Poor Katey had cause for her grief. As she sat up in their poor bed, nursing her baby, and shivering with cold and misery, the light fell on Jerry's face – a changed face to her – for on it was still the remains of a stupid frown, and the old firmness of the mouth had not yet returned. For the first time she noticed the cut on her husband's head, and with a cry, suppressed lest it should wake him, bent over to look at it. She was terribly frightened, for she had not had even a suspicion that he had been hurt. Now, having placed her baby beside her, she made a careful examination, and was horrified at the appearance which the wound presented. It

was carefully dressed, but the very carefulness of the dressing increased her fear, for she should not see the actual
extent of the wound, but could only fear, and of course she
feared the worst. So she watched and waited till the morning
light grew clearer and clearer, and then at his usual hour
Jerry awoke.

There are different ways of waking, and those who take
the trouble to study the matter can see for themselves how
much good or evil conscience has to do with it. Jerry awoke
with an evil conscience, that which makes 'cowards of us all,'
and as the whole of yesterday, with its temptation, yielded to
and its last prolonged debauch, rushed back upon his mind,
he covered his eyes with his hands to shut out the reproach
which he felt should be in the eyes of his wife. Katey saw the
motion and understood it, and it wrung her heart with a
bitter pain. She put her arms round his neck and said, with
the tenderness that can only be in the voice of a loving wife
exercising the sweet woman's virtue of forgiveness:

'Oh, Jerry, Jerry, don't turn from me. Look to me, Jerry,
dear. Can you find love and comfort anywhere but in the
heart of your wife.'

Jerry could not look her in the face, but blindly groping,
as if in the dark, he put his arms round her and hid his face
in her bosom.

Neither spoke for a while, but Katey rocked his head on
her breast, as a while ago she had rocked her baby's. Presently she said:

'Don't speak, Jerry, not one word to me. Let me dress your
poor hurt head, and then you can go to your work amongst
your mates, knowing that there is no cloud between us.'

Jerry raised his head and looked at her, with his eyes full
of honest tears and his mouth with something of the old
firmness. He held her from him, at arm's length, in a loving
way, and said, slowly:

'Katey, I have done wrong. Don't speak. I must say it, for
it is true; but I hope it will be the last time. Trust me this
once, and you won't have more cause for fear.'

He did not wish her to answer, and so she stayed silent.

All that day Jerry worked very hard, and resisted all
temptations, both those from within – for his excess of the

night before had parched him – and those from his friends; and he went home that night to Katey with a good conscience.

The next day was the same, and the next, and the next. Thus his old confidence in himself came back to him: 'Ye that stand take heed lest ye fall.' With his confidence came a temptation to do things to test it, and conscious of his own strength of purpose, Jerry went across to Grinnell's 'just to prove,' he thought to himself, 'that I am not afraid.'

Great efforts were made by those present, who included Mons, Sebright, and Popham, to induce him to take something, but he consistently refused, but with good humour. Still he felt it pleasant to be in a cheerful room amongst a lot of companions, much better than grubbing away at piles of wood grimy with the dust of months, and he thought that now that he felt how strong he was he would often take a run across the road and hear some of the gossip of the day between his spells of work.

These days were pleasant for Katey, for she saw that Jerry was quite his old self, and she was beginning to get reconciled to the new life. Jerry never told her of his visits to Grinnell's, for he thought to himself, 'What is the use of telling her. There is no harm in it, but she will only be imagining harm, and worrying herself about nothing.'

Sebright came to see him one evening. Katey made her husband's friend welcome, as every good wife does. The two men chatted pleasantly, Katey occasionally joining in. She saw that Jerry enjoyed the evening, and she herself, devoid as she was of friends, enjoyed it too, and asked their guest to come again. He was not a man to stand on ceremony in such matters, and he did come again, and his visits grew more frequent till at last his coming was a matter to be expected every second night or so.

Mons also paid a visit, and was made welcome, and repeated his visits also. Katey did not like either man, but she disliked the latter. She had known Sebright long ago, and he had at least the title of old acquaintanceship to be liked; but Mons was a newcomer, and one that she felt was, for her husband's sake, not to be encouraged.

Thus things went on for some time. Occasionally letters

came from Dublin telling of the progress of affairs. At last
Katey received one, which she opened with some curiosity, as
the writing was not familiar to her. It ran as follows:–*

'Dear Mrs Katey – I have some news to tell you wh you
will be glad to hear. I am going to be married. You will never
guess who to, wh is Miss M'Anaspie, who I met at your home.
Margaret – that is, Miss M'Anaspie, desires me to say she
hopes you're well, and that my young god-son or god-daugh-
ter, or whatever the brat is, is quite well. I hope some day to
be something else but a *god*-father. [Here was inserted in a
feminine hand – 'Don't mind him; he is a wretch.'] We, wh we
is I and Margaret – Miss M'Anaspie – are going over to
London on our honeymoon, and hope to see you. Margaret –
Miss M'Anaspie – says you are sure to live in some wretched
hole, but you will not mind us going if we don't; provided,
Margaret – Miss M'Anaspie – says that her new clothes won't
get spoiled by going upstairs like a corkscrew to a garret, or
down a slippery ladder into a cellar, where your head knocks
above you in the grating, and your feet slip and you fall
amongst the oysters, and shrimps, and prawns. But we will
go all the same. Wishing you all the good wishes wh you
wish – in which I join [written in a female hand again] – we
remain, dear madam, yours respectfully.

'John Muldoon.
'PS – I hope Jerry hasn't taken to drinking yet.'

This letter made poor Katey very unhappy. There was in
it a tone of selfish heartlessness which would have made its
contents a matter of indifference only for two or three of the
remarks it contained.

'What right have they,' Katey thought indignantly, 'to
think that Jerry would take to drinking? "Has he taken to it
yet," indeed, as if Jerry would be a drunkard? My Jerry, that
never was drunk but once, and that never goes near a public-
house now. And why did they think we lived in a garret, or a
cellar either. I'll be bound there isn't as clean or as comfortable a room in John Muldoon's house as this very room. It's

---

*   Spelling and punctuation in this letter are taken from *The Shamrock*.

like their impudence.' And so ran on the little woman's thoughts till something within her whispered, 'Pride, Katey, pride. Take care of pride. Keep your room clean and nice, and it won't matter whether they think you live in a garret or anywhere else.'

In time Mr and Mrs Muldoon came over to London, and, after sending a message to Katey that she might be prepared, they paid her a visit. Mrs Muldoon was radiant with every colour in the rainbow, and from the number of garments floating and flying about her looked of such portentous dimensions that her little stout husband seemed like a dwarf.

John Muldoon, however, did not consider himself a dwarf by any means, and was as proud of his wife 'as a dog with a tin tail.' Mrs Muldoon was most patronisingly affectionate as became her exalted rank and her blushing condition. She kissed Katey several times, and disported herself with the children, whom she took turn about on her knees until she got tired of them.

Her conduct towards the baby was worthy of note. Towards it she displayed an amount of affectionate curiosity worthy of all praise. She dandled it in her hands, she kissed it, she cuddled it, she almost strangled it, and by her unskilful nursing managed to inflict on it much pain in the way of pins.

Katey stood by, now smiling, now anxious, as the child seemed pleased or unhappy.

Suddenly, without any apparent cause, Mrs Muldoon stood up and said –

'John, dear, I think we have stayed a long time. Mrs Katey will want to get back to her work.' And so, taking her husband's arm, went away, after a hurried farewell.

Katey was distressed, for she feared there was some offence, and the tone adopted by her new relative was gall and wormwood to her womanly feelings. For they had not wished to see Jerry, but merely asked for him. It was only, however, that the bride was tired of the visit, and wished to see some more of the sights of London.

A letter came from Parnell one day which gave Katey great pleasure. One sentence in it ran as follows:– 'Never

forget that you must be your husband's Guardian Angel in
case he falls into any temptation. Above all things remember
that your hold on him is stronger while there is perfect
confidence. When there is between man and wife a shadow of
suspicion or doubt – when either hesitates to tell a secret or
confess a fault, not knowing how it may be received – then
there is over their lives the shadow of a dark future. Never
keep a secret, then, except when it is not your own, from
your husband, and strive so to act that he conceal nothing
from you.'

As she read this the little woman said to herself with a
mixture of pride and thoughtfulness –

'There are no secrets between Jerry and me, thank God.
Sure there isn't a thought of my heart I wouldn't tell him,
and I know that he tells me everything.'

This thought tended to perfect the happiness which, now
that Jerry was going along so steadily and prosperously, was
her natural condition.

A few evenings after, whilst Jerry was at the theatre,
Sebright came in. In the course of conversation he happened
to mention Grinnell's name.

'Who is Grinnell?' asked Katey.

'Don't you know Grinnell? Why he is a friend of Jerry's.'

'A friend of Jerry's! how odd that he never mentioned him
to me. What is he?'

'He keeps the public-house opposite the stage door of the
Stanley.'

Katey's heart seemed to turn to stone, but she did not
choose to let Sebright see her feeling lest it should do harm,
and so, for the present, let the matter drop.

When her visitor had gone she was in a dreadful state of
mind. She longed to cry with a bitter longing, but feared to,
lest Jerry should find her eyes red on his return from work,
and so she bravely bore her sorrow – the sorrow that followed the thought of her husband's concealment.

When Jerry returned he found her bright and cheerful as
usual, and in a talking humour. He had had a hard and long
day's work, and was now quite in a humour for a quiet chat.
Katey had been thinking over Sebright's remark, and had
come to the conclusion that as Jerry had not told her about

Grinnell he had some object in his concealment, and that to force a confession would be to put him in the wrong at the very outset. Accordingly she began her conversation, with the object of trying to invite his confidence.

After talking over the state of things at the theatre, to which she had been several times, Jerry's companions, and daily life, she asked him –

'What do you do all the evening, Jerry? It must be very slow work for you.'

'Well, it's slow at times; but, as a rule, there's plenty to do. So that with looking after the cellars, and the flies, and the wings, and trying to keep the men square and sober, my time isn't idle I can tell you.'

'Is it hard to keep the men sober?'

'Isn't it. They'd be always over in Grinnell's if I let them.'

'What is Grinnell's?'

'A public-house over the way.'

'And is Grinnell the proprietor?'

'He is, and a good fellow too – very pleasant and sociable.'

Jerry was thinking that the present was a good time to tell his wife that he sometimes went in, but did not drink anything; but such a look of fear came over her face, despite all her efforts, that he did not care to go on, and hastily turned aside the current of conversation.

Katey felt that the shadow was growing, but yet feared to say anything more at present lest Jerry should be hurt.

Poor little woman; she was in great doubt, pitiable doubt, and as she had no one near to advise her, was driven almost into despair. In her perplexity she wrote to Parnell a tender little letter, full of love for her husband, and asking earnestly for advice. The answer came in a way that she did not expect, for one day, shortly after, whilst she was busily engaged over her washing-tub a tall man, none other than Parnell himself, walked in.

Katey looked at him in amazement, and gave a low, glad cry, and, as she was, without even thinking of her wet hands and arms, ran over and put her arms round his neck and kissed him.

Whilst she was in this attitude Jerry came in, and, seeing his wife with her arms round a man's neck, for he did not at

first recognise Parnell – not expecting to see him – gave vent
to an indignant 'Hullo!'

Parnell turned his head round, and Katey peeped over his
shoulder at her husband. When Jerry saw who it was he
nearly shook his hand off and pressed him into a chair,
asking him all sorts of questions, without giving him time to
reply.

Parnell told him all the Dublin news; amongst other
things giving him a description of Muldoon's wedding, at
which they all laughed heartily.

When dinner was over, Jerry had to hurry back to his
work, and Parnell remained to talk with Katey.

Katey did not delay, but proceeded to tell her trouble in
full, Parnell listening quietly, and looking very grave. When
she had finished, he took her hand in his and said –

'I do not like Jerry's keeping back anything from you, but
this matter will be all right, I hope and believe.'

He was interrupted by the voice of the landlady calling
out, 'Mrs O'Sullivan, here's a boy wants you to go down to
the theatre as quick as ever you can, something has
happened.'

Katey, with a deadly fear in her heart, hurried with
Parnell down to the theatre.

7

Katey's Trials

When Jerry had arrived at the theatre he had found visitors waiting to see him. They were none other than Mr and Mrs Muldoon, who had appeared just before. The bride had taken a fancy to see the inside of the theatre in which Jerry worked; and being certain of finding him at his business, the pair had come straight to the theatre instead of calling at his lodgings.

A man is seldom so busy that he cannot spare a while to act as cicerone to his friends; and Jerry accordingly laid aside his hurry, and conducted the happy couple over the theatre. Both husband and wife took a great pleasure in everything, and insisted in going everywhere. Margaret would work the machines by which in the stage art the sounds of rain and wind and thunder are produced; and altogether the pair raised as pretty a storm as had been heard in the theatre for many a long day.

In spite of her prejudice against going up corkscrew stairs and down into cellars, Mrs Muldoon managed to poke her nose into every odd corner of the stage. She insisted on going up into the flies, where the dust lay in places almost inches thick, quite heedless of the state of dirt to which her clothing was reduced. This part of the sight-seeing did not please her husband much on account of several accidents which happened to him. In the first place, he slipped on a flight of stairs as steep as a ladder and 'barked' his shin. Then he ran his head against a beam and utterly destroyed his new silk hat. Finally, he put his foot in a division between two boards and hurt his ankle, narrowly escaping a sprain. At all these calamities his wife laughed loudly except at the spoiling of the hat, for which she reprimanded him severely as being guilty of a needless piece of extravagance. Mr Muldoon began

to think that married life was not such a delightful thing
after all.

Then they all went down to the cellars, as Mrs Muldoon
wanted to see how the demons came up through the ground.
Jerry explained to her the mechanism of the traps, how a
sliding board was pulled away so as to leave an open space,
into which fitted exactly a piece of flooring, on which stood
the person or thing to be raised; that to this flooring were
attached ropes which worked over pulleys and were attached
to immense counter-weights, which, when suddenly released,
shot up the trap swiftly between its grooves. Mrs Muldoon
wished to see it working, so Jerry drew away the slot, and
released the counter-weights. She gave a little ecstatic laugh
as the trap flew up, and then said to Jerry –

'But surely it doesn't work that way when there's anything on it?'

'Just the same.'

'And how do you go up? Do you just stand on that and
then up you go?'

'Exactly.'

'How do they stand? I suppose as stiff as pokers?'

'This way,' said Jerry, getting up and standing on the trap.

This was just what Mrs Muldoon wanted. She had all
along been watching for an opportunity of releasing the trap,
and had purposely led Jerry to stand on it that she might see
him shoot up through the opening in the stage. Without
giving him warning she suddenly released the trap, which
flew up. Jerry, to whom the experience was novel, for his
business was to work the trap and not ascend on it, felt the
ground flying up with him, and was horribly startled, for the
idea of the trap working of its own accord never entered his
head. With an instinctive movement he started back, and in
doing so lost his balance. He was hurled against the groove
in which the trap worked, and from the velocity with which
he was moving received a desperate blow.

When the trap was closed, Jerry lay on it perfectly insensible, and bleeding profusely.

In the meantime Mr Muldoon had been prowling about
the cellar in a very bad humour, looking at the various appliances. When the trap flew up Margaret saw that Jerry was

hurt, but did not know how much. She got afraid of something serious, and wished to avoid the consequences.
Accordingly she ran over to her husband and said hurriedly –

'John, dear, I think Jerry has hurt himself. He was
standing on the trap and it flew up, and he struck something. They will lay the blame on us. Don't you think we had
better go?'

'All right, but make haste,' said the husband. And so they
found their way with some difficulty into the street.

There was no one on the stage at the time, so Jerry's
accident was unnoticed. He lay there for some time, still
senseless, and still bleeding, till Mr Griffin saw him as he
crossed the stage on his way to his own room. He thought it
was a case of drunkenness and turned the man over with his
foot, with that contemptuous 'get up' which is used on such
occasions. As he did so he saw the blood, and with an exclamation, bent over to look more closely. He saw that some
accident had occurred and called for help. In a few moments
the various employés began turning up, one by one, till quite
a little crowd had assembled; the alarm penetrated to
Grinnell's and a large contingent arrived from that quarter.

Jerry's head was raised and the restoratives usual to such
occasions applied, but all in vain. Accordingly, a doctor was
sent for, and a boy despatched to tell Mrs O'Sullivan.

Katey and Parnell arrived before the doctor. When the
former saw her husband, limp and senseless, with his pale
face looking vacantly upward from the knees of the man who
was supporting his head, and the stage floor round him
stained with blood, she gave a low, startled scream, which
subsided into a prolonged moan. For an instant or two she
stood, as if petrified, holding her arms out – surprise in her
attitude and terror in her looks. Then, with a little hoarse,
sibilant moan, she drew her left hand across her eyes and
forehead, as if to clear her brain and sight, and then she
knelt beside her husband for an instant, with her hands
tightly clenched. The crowd made way for her and stood a
little aloof.

When she recovered her shock sufficiently to understand
what was before her, poor Katey's grief was terrible. She
threw herself on the body of her husband and passed her

hands over his hands, his face, his hair, his bosom, whispering in a low, heartbreaking voice:

'Jerry, Jerry, wake up; speak to me, Jerry, dear. Oh, Jerry, won't you speak to me – to Katey, your wife, – your little wife that loves you? Oh, *weirasthru, weirasthru*,* he's dead, he's dead! He won't speak to me. He'll never speak to me, again. Oh, Jerry, Jerry, *asthore!*** – Jerry, Jerry.'

The poor little woman's voice died away into a long moan, as she buried her face in the bosom of her husband and wept.

Many of those standing round were touched, and turned away their heads not to show their emotion. All were silent, and waited.

The arrival of the doctor created a diversion. He was a fussy, good-humoured little man, who always looked at the bright side of things. His natural impulse on seeing a woman give way to violent grief was to think that it was without cause; and, as his impulse was supported by his experience, he generally continued so to think. When he bustled in and saw Katey stretched on the body of her husband, he spoke –

'Come, come! what is all this? Who is crying? The man's wife? Then the man's wife has no right to cry. It is an insult to me – to science. The man's wife thinks, I suppose, that Providence is very hard on her. What right, I say, has the man's wife to judge Providence before science has spoken. The man is sure not to be dead. Why, the man's wife ought to be ashamed of herself for not being thankful that he is not killed. Stand away and let me see the man, and we'll very soon hear the man's wife laughing instead of crying.'

While he was speaking he was preparing to make an examination of Jerry.

Katey was cheered by his tone, and stood up, anxious to the last degree, but feeling somewhat ashamed of her hasty grief.

The doctor made the examination usual in such cases, and then stood up before he spoke. Katey watched his lips to tell by their motion the coming words before they could be spoken.

---

* This was spelled 'wirrasthrue' on p.43, but should be 'wirrasthru'.

** *asthore* – (Irish) darling or sweetheart.

'Just as I thought.' Katey's heart gave a great bound of joy, and her head began to reel, so that she seemed to hear the remainder of his speech as through a curtain. 'Now look at the man's wife – she is going to faint, I warrant, just when she ought to be calm. That's right. Courage, my poor girl, your husband is only stunned, and will be able to put his arms round your neck in ten minutes.'

Katey's faintness began to pass away, and she knelt down by Jerry ready to do the doctor's bidding. The latter gave some directions, which were carried out, and after a while Jerry opened his eyes. For a time he did not remember anything, and seemed quite dazed, staring blankly at the crowd of faces which he saw around him. Presently he recovered sufficiently to answer the doctor's questions, which elicited the fact that he was hurt in the head and the side. His wounds were dressed, and Katey, after receiving instructions as to his treatment, took him home, with Parnell's assistance, in a cab.

Parnell was obliged to return to Dublin that night; and as Jerry was very feverish and restless, Katey was obliged to sit up with him all night. In the morning Jerry was worse, and seemed to be a little off his head. He did not seem to realise where he was, and answered Katey's anxious inquiries so strangely that she got frightened and sent for Dr Sharp, in whom she had acquired great confidence from his manner at the time of the accident.

When he saw Jerry Dr Sharp looked very grave. Katey saw his face fall and began to cry. He turned on her severely and said, although with a spice of tenderness through his sternness –

'Silence, woman. This is no time to cry. This is a time to act – time enough to cry when there is a reason for it.'

'Oh, doctor, is he very bad?' asked poor Katey, so anxiously that the doctor patted her on the head as he answered:–

'It is best for you to face the worse, my dear. The wound on his head is worse than I thought. I think he will have an attack of brain fever. There now, I oughtn't to tell you anything. Come, come, stir yourself, and then you won't want to faint. We must get him to hospital whilst he is fit to be moved.'

At the word hospital Katey's fear became deadly, for she looked upon an institution as in some wise synonymous with ruin; but the doctor was peremptory, and before she had time to mourn Jerry was safely lodged in the nearest hospital.

Katey would have stayed with him all day only that she had her children to look after. Her sorrow at leaving him was much mitigated by the fact that one of the nurses, a Sister of Mercy, with whose sweet gentle face she fell in love, had promised to give him unfailing attention.

When she got home and thought of its desolation, now temporary, but perhaps to be permanent – Katey would have willingly cried herself stupid. But she felt that she must not give way to her feelings; the children were sobbing bitterly, having missed her for so long; and she felt, moreover, that now during Jerry's illness, which might be a protracted one, there devolved on her the entire support of the family.

When she was going to bed that night she knelt down to say her prayers with a sadder heart than she had ever had before; she prayed for help and strength, and made a silent vow that she would work unceasingly and uncomplainingly, so that all might be as of old for Jerry when he should be well.

Nobly she kept her vow. Early and late she toiled, her only times of relaxation being those which she spent in the hospital watching by her husband's bedside with her heart wrung by his piteous moans. He did not know her, and thus wrung her heart still more. To a loving wife there is scarcely anything so painful as the knowing that the man she loves – who is a part of herself – does not know her – that the twain which were one, are now but twain again.

She found it easy enough to get work at first, for some of the people living near knowing of her misfortune held out a helping hand. There was not much to gain, for the neighbourhood was a wretched one, but what little was came freely.

It is amongst the very poor that true generosity is found. The rich man pours his gifts, large to magnificence it may be, into the treasury, but he gives them from his superfluity: it is not often that he has to deny himself in order to be even lavish. But the mite of the widow comes out of her distress, and is valued accordingly. It would give many a wholesome lesson to even the truly charitable rich to see and know the good deeds which are done by their poorer brethren. It is only amongst the poor that charity will tolerate equality – nay, where is accorded the dignity which is the birthright of misfortune.

Katey got some little help from Dublin from Mrs O'Sullivan, who, however, was unable to do much for her on account of the absconding of a solicitor to whom she had intrusted all her little savings.

After a little while the work began to fall away; and do what she would poor Katey found it hard to keep the wolf from the door. She was up before daylight and into the market to buy vegetables which she then sold from house to house; she went charring; she tried needlework. Everything by which an honest penny could be turned she tried, and found no degradation in any employment no matter how lowly.

At last the constant working and watching tended, together with her anxiety, to make her so weak that she could hardly work. Jerry was still dangerously ill. He had by this time regained his consciousness, and she had the pleasure each day of hearing his voice speaking sweet words to her. But he was still wretchedly helpless, and she knew that it would be many a long day before he had regained his old vigour. She did not let him know of her work, but managed to let him believe that the help which she was getting from his mother was sufficient to keep her and the children from want.

When her strength began to go, many articles which could be dispensed with had to go too. Katey's first visit to a pawn-office was a bitter experience. She was afraid and ashamed to go alone, and got her landlady, from whom she borrowed a thick veil, to go with her. She bore the ordeal well enough, but when she came home she burst out crying, and took her children on her lap and wept over them and clasped them convulsively to her arms.

Her first visit was not her last; and by the time that Jerry was discharged from hospital their lodging, now reduced to a single room, was denuded of all the articles of luxury which had once been Katey's pride, and even of those articles of utility which were not necessary.

It was with a sinking heart that Katey took home her husband, and it was a moment of agony to her when Jerry looked around him in bewilderment, searching with wondering eyes for all the objects which were familiar to him. Jerry was thunderstruck. For a time he stood silent, and then asked as does one in a dream –

'Why, Katey, what's all this? Where is everything gone to? I don't seem to understand.'

Katey was silent, thinking what to say. Jerry asked again with that irritability which often accompanies extreme physical prostration –

'Why don't you answer me? It isn't kind to keep me waiting.'

Katey burst into tears. Her feelings and her strength had been too long tried, and now on this day, which she had hoped and prayed for, when her husband had been restored to her, that he should accuse her of unkindness was too much. Jerry got still more impatient, and spoke crossly.

'Katey, what do you mean by crying when I ask you a question? Have I done any wrong to you? Perhaps it would be better if I had died.'

Katey cried still more bitterly, and could only murmur as she laid her head on her husband's shoulder –

'Oh, Jerry, Jerry. Oh, Jerry, Jerry.'

He put her aside with a motion rather of impatience than of unkindness. Katey did not distinguish the difference; with her head bent down she did not see his face, but merely felt the motion, and her sorrow turned into a wail.

'Oh, Jerry, Jerry, Jerry, Jerry, that ever the day should come when you should put me from you, and after all I've suffered. Oh-h-h, oh-h-h, oh-h-h,' and she moaned as one in dire pain.

Jerry threw himself back in his chair, and said, with a kind of desperation –

'Oh, go on, go on. Cry away, and make me and yourself miserable. Would to God I had died, and then you might have been more cheerful.'

Katey heard no more, she fainted.

8

Down the Hill

From that hour a cloud seemed to have settled between Jerry O'Sullivan and his wife. Katey did all in her power to atone for what seemed in Jerry's eyes to be a piece of petulance, but which she knew to be the result of nervous weakness springing from protracted suffering and overwork. Jerry, as he got a little stronger too, got less petulant, and did not resist Katey's advances, although there seemed to be still in his breast a sense of injury which took the outward expression of a kind of latent antagonism, specially galling to his wife. It was a good while before he was able to work; and neither his strength nor temper was improved by finding that during his illness his place at the theatre had been given away to another man. When he was able he called to the theatre, and after waiting for a long time, saw the manager, who coolly told him that of course he could not afford to pay two men for doing the same work, and so had been obliged to get another tradesman.

Jerry remonstrated, saying that he did not wish to take away any man's bread, but that after all, fair play was fair play, and that as he had been injured in the theatre he thought he should be treated with some consideration, and be restored to his place which he had done nothing to forfeit. He was met with the answer, that a man must bear the risk and trouble of his own accidents on his own shoulders; that the manager had not been to blame in the matter; that Jerry had had the working of the machinery entirely under his own control, and that it was his own fault if anything went wrong.

Jerry felt that there was a *soupçon* of justice in this, and said no more. Indeed he did not get the chance of speaking, as the manager walked away. He did not know how the

accident had occurred, for the idea of Mrs Muldoon's part in
it never entered his head. He took it for granted that it was
one of those accidents 'which will occur,' and hard as was his
lot, that he must put up with it.

He tried to get work in the neighbourhood, but there was
then in London a strike in the building trade, and there was
no work to be had. Day after day, Jerry walked for miles and
miles, trying every place to get work, but all in vain. He had
not yet recovered his strength, and so felt his efforts
cramped, and consequently worried himself so much, and
fretted so constantly, that both his health and his temper
suffered.

Katey had much to bear. Since Jerry was earning nothing, she had to earn for all. She worked early and late, and
grudged herself even a sufficiency of food that Jerry might
have enough and so get stronger. She was always in good
humour, and no matter what pain or sorrow was in her heart
there was ever a loving smile to meet Jerry when either he
or she returned home. Still she could not earn enough to buy
sufficient food, and so the pawn-office was visited again and
again, till the home was left well nigh empty.

At last Jerry, finding that no work at his trade could be
obtained, made up his mind to do what he could. He tried to
get work in different places and of different kinds, but, like
many another poor fellow, he found that London is too full of
hungry mouths for work to go long a-begging, and it seemed
to him that his lot in life was to be for the future just too late
to get anything he sought for. One day he thought he would
try the theatre, for he knew work, though of poor kind, was
sometimes to be got there. It was not without a mighty effort
that he made up his mind to seek employment from the man
who had superseded him, and whom in his heart he regarded
bitterly as an usurper. The new man seemed to recognise
and to reciprocate the hostility, and his manner to poor Jerry
was extremely galling. He was happy to be able to show his
own power by giving work to the other man, and by patron-
izing him, or else he would have peremptorily refused. As it
was he gave him some work, and even made a point of
seeming to treat him differently from the other men who
were doing the same work – a fact which made every one of

them hate Jerry with the hatred of jealousy.

The little he now earned helped to banish the extreme want from the household, yet somehow all seemed now even more miserable than when dire cold and hunger stared them in the face. The cause was this. While cold and hunger, and dire misery were inmates of the house there was something to be borne – there was a sense of complete difference between the old circumstances and the present, altogether a sense that this through which they were passing was unreal – merely a crisis – and that the present evils must pass away in time. But now no such sense of contrast existed. Jerry was working as of old, and enough money was coming in to buy off the officers of the grim sheriff, Death. Jerry was working, indeed, but not in the old way. There was now neither hope nor ambition. To work was merely to toil ceaselessly to support existence that was a burden.

Jerry grew more and more despondent as the days wore on. Katey's bright looks and hopeful words were now of no avail, and slowly and surely the conviction grew on her that sorrow, hopeless and overwhelming, was coming into their lives. Jerry began to feel, in all its force, how great had been his folly in leaving Dublin. Whilst he worked he kept thinking to himself, how different all would have been had he remained at home. Here sickness and trouble would have been his surest titles to the help and sympathy of his many friends; but in London, amid strangers where the maxim of life seemed to be *sauve qui peut* – a maxim which might be translated 'Every man for himself' – all was different, and to be down in the world was to be trampled upon.

Whenever he thought thus, there came to Jerry a fierce temptation to lose sight of his misery as other men lost sight of theirs – in that hell-cauldron, which is picturesquely termed 'the bowl.' He resisted this temptation for a time, but he felt that his resolution was giving way. He would have returned to Dublin but for lack of means, and he had not yet fallen so low as to beg for assistance.

One day he was reprimanded in good round terms by his superior for some seeming fault. He answered temperately, and was told to 'shut up.' He did shut up, for he felt that he dared not risk his present employment.

That day at dinner hour he went to Grinnell's and drank recklessly. When a man who resists temptation for a time suddenly gives way to it, his fall is mighty. Jerry was unable to return to his work, and after a drunken sleep in the tap-room was left at home in the evening still half stupefied.

Katey saw what had happened; and none can imagine her anguish save those who have known and felt some terrible sorrow – some sorrow where there was no thought of self. She did not wish for death, because she thought of her children; but too surely she saw that Jerry had been drinking to drown his care, and she knew that till the care disappeared – which could now only be at death – the remedy would be attempted again and again.

And she was right. Shakspere was right, too, when he wrote –

'Lilies that fester smell far worse than weeds.'

When a naturally good disposition is warped or bent in a wrong direction all the strength that had been for good works now for evil; and in proportion to the natural strength of character is the speediness of the complete ruin. Day after day Jerry visited Grinnell's, and day by day he grew more of a sot. He very seldom got drunk, because he felt that such would involve his dismissal; but he was nearly always in a state of 'fuddle.'

Katey's life grew harder and harder to bear, but she strove ever with herself, and determined that no effort, active or passive, either of action or endurance, should be wanting on her part to reclaim her husband. She used to wait up for Jerry no matter what hour he stayed out till, and never made his coming home unpleasant by showing that she had been sitting up or suffering anxiety from his absence.

A couple of times when she thought it likely that she would see him she peeped through the door of Grinnell's, and each time saw Jerry either drinking or playing cards, or following both pursuits at once. The gambling was a new phase of vice to her, for she did not know that the one sin follows hard on the track of the other.

DOWN THE HILL

Jerry had, indeed, gone down the hill. With no friends round him to arrest his downward course, but surrounded by a troop of evil companions who wished to see him as low or lower than themselves, he was falling, falling still. At such times Katey had stood shivering in the doorway, shrinking out into the night each time anyone entered the house or left it, but coming back again and again as if fascinated. She noticed that Jerry in his play seemed to have always bad luck, and to always play recklessly. It was heartbreaking work to her standing thus an unseen witness of the fall of the man she loved better than herself, and oftentimes the temptation to go in and try to induce him to leave the place became almost too strong for her. She retained herself, however, overcome for the time by the deadly fear that any overt act of hers might shear away the last thread of her influence over him.

At last one evening the temptation to enter became too strong. Jerry had seemingly worse luck than usual, and drank more accordingly. He got exceedingly quarrelsome, and before anyone could interfere a fight had arisen. It was not a long fight, for the bystanders were numerous, and soon choked off the combatants the way men choke off fighting dogs.

Jerry's opponent – none other than Sebright – regained command of his temper in a few seconds; but as for Jerry himself, his rage was frightful. He would not be pacified or appeased in any way, but continued to rage and storm with purple swollen face and voice hoarse from passion and drink. Katey saw that they were making him worse by holding him the way they did, and irritating him. She could stand it no longer. She pushed open the door and entered.

At the sound of the opening door all turned round in fear that the newcomer was a policeman, and in the universal movement Jerry was released. Seeing a pretty young woman enter – for Katey, despite her long spell of hardship and suffering, was a pretty young woman still – the men who did not know her began what they called 'being civil.' Jerry knew instinctively that Katey would not have entered the public-house without some cause, and his conscience told him that that cause was his own misconduct; and so in his semi-drunken rage he determined to vent his anger, which was half for himself, on her. In addition, he heard the *sotto voce* remarks of the other men, and this inflamed him still more. He came angrily forward, and said to his wife in hard, stern angry tones –

'What brings you here?'

The suddenness of the question, and the tone of it, took Katey by surprise, and she had to pause before replying. Her embarrassment was increased by the glare of light, and the rude admiring eyes turned upon her.

Jerry repeated his question with his face inflamed and his right hand raised. It was the first time Jerry's hand had ever been raised to her in anger, and it was no wonder that poor Katey covered her face and wept. This seemed to make Jerry more angry still. He took her by the arm roughly, and shook her, saying –

'At it again. Cryin' – always cryin'.' Then, again, with a sudden change, 'What brings you here, I say – what brings you here?'

Katey lifted her head, and looked at him pleadingly through her tears. 'Come home, Jerry; come home.'

'I'll not go home. Go you home and don't dare to watch or follow me again. Out of this, I say – out of this.'

'Oh, Jerry, Jerry, don't send me away to-night. Oh, Jerry, you're hurting me; indeed you are. I'll go quietly. Do let me go, Jerry. Look at all the men. It is ashamed of my life I am.'

'Out of this, I say.'

'Oh, Jerry, come home.'

For answer Jerry lifted his hand and struck her in the face. The blow was a severe one, but Katey did not seem to feel it. The pain in her heart at the spirit which prompted the blow was so great that no outward pain would have touched her for the moment. With the courage and resolution of utter despair – for what could now be worse since Jerry had struck her – she clung to him, crying almost wildly –

'Come home, come home.'

Jerry dashed her aside, and ran over to the counter.

'Give me brandy,' he said to Grinnell, 'quick, man, give me brandy.'

Grinnell was in nowise backward, and gave him as he desired. He drank off two or three glasses one after the other despite all Katey could do to prevent him.

After this his coming home was a matter of mere labour, for he got too drunk to stand or to think, and lay on the floor like a log.

Katey looked round appealingly for help. Sebright and Mons, the only two men whom she knew, had both disappeared, for both of them retained sufficient pride to make them anxious to avoid the gaze of the injured woman. The help came from an unexpected quarter. Grinnell, who had hitherto been leaning complacently across the bar, came from behind it, and said very gently –

'Let me help you.'

Katey was so anxious about Jerry that she did not notice the strangeness of the offer coming from such a man, but answered gratefully –

'Oh, thank you, sir. God will bless you.'

Grinnell smiled softly to himself, but Katey did not see the smile.

The pot-boy was sent for a cab, and, when it came, was

put in charge of the bar, whilst Grinnell helped Katey to take home her husband. There was lots of assistance to put him into the cab, but, as she could not get him out herself, Grinnell went with her himself. When the vehicle began to move, Grinnell said softly –

'This is a very sad affair.'

'Oh, sad indeed,' sighed Katey.

'I wish to God,' said Grinnell, with intensity of voice, 'that I had known of you before. Your husband would not have got drink in my house.'

'God bless you, sir, for these words. Oh, you will help me to keep him straight now, will you not?'

'I will.'

'You see,' said Katey, feeling that a palliation of her husband's conduct was necessary, 'the poor fellow has had much trouble and sorrow, and he was badly treated at the theatre.'

'I know it – I know it,' said Grinnell, with indignation. 'Didn't the whole neighbourhood ring with it, and the people cry shame on old Meredith. Why, I couldn't stand it, and it was no business of mine. I only wished to see justice. I amn't so bad as I look. I went to him, and says I – "Look you here, sir," says I, "you're doin' wrong. Here's the best workman in London, and the best fellow, too," says I, "and you're losin' him and doin' a wrong thing. And don't you expect to gain by it," says I, "for wickedness never prospers," says I, "and I tell you what," says I, "some of the other theatres will get hold of him, and then won't you be sorry. I have a good deal of influence," says I, "and I'll use it all for him" ' –

He was going on thus when the cab stopped. He helped Katey to lift out Jerry, and between them they carried him up to the room.

Grinnell waited a few minutes only, and said good night to Katey in a most friendly manner.

'I will call round in the morning and see how he goes on,' he said, 'and if you want anything that I have, you know it is quite at your disposal.'

'Oh, sir, I wouldn't for the world. I have no money, and I wouldn't for the world have Jerry feel that I owed money for anything.'

Grinnell gave a sudden unintentional laugh. 'Don't yon fret about that,' he said. 'O'Sullivan owes me myself too much money already to let that trouble him.'

Katey put her hand on her heart at this fresh blow, but said nothing.

Grinnell went on:

'But that doesn't matter. Lord bless you. He's as welcome as the flowers of May. I'm too fond of him to let a trifle of money vex him.' Then he went out.

Katey, despite her prejudice, could not but feel better disposed towards him. The narrative of what he had done for Jerry in going to the manager, touched her deeply, and she said to herself:–

'Well, we should never judge by appearances. It is a lesson to us.'

Had she known that in all Grinnell had said there was not one single word of truth, she might have thought differently.

9

The Trail of the Serpent

Katey watched by her husband for a long time till at last she cried herself to sleep. Her sleep was troubled by horrid dreams of care and sorrow, and nameless and formless horrors. She did not wake however. When we dream thus of awful things, and do not wake, the effect is much more wearing on the nervous system than if we did; and so in the morning when Katey woke she felt chilled and miserable. She started up, and in the half-light of the early morning found that she was alone. Jerry had waked early, and had hurriedly got up, struck with remorse when he remembered the previous evening, and not daring to meet the face of his wife. Katey was at once in deadly fear, for her woman's weakness prompted thoughts of terrible possibilities. She got up quickly and went down into the street.

She looked right and left for any sign of him, and after wavering between them finally with an instinct, pitiful since it had such a genesis, took her way towards Grinnell's, feeling that she would find her husband there.

Her instinct was not deceived. When she peeped in through the door of the public-house she saw Jerry standing by the bar with a glass in his hand, which Grinnell was filling. A man does not hold his glass in such a way unless it is being refilled, and this poor Katey knew by instinct. She shuddered as she looked – for she saw that Jerry was drinking to get drunk quickly.

Indeed it was a sorry and a pitiful picture – one which man or woman with a human heart in their bosom would shudder to see. In the grey light of the wintry morning the working man with clothing tossed, and hair unkempt – with feverous look and bloodshot eyes, drinking his rum at a draught, and taking it from the hand of one who, with soiled finery and unwashed face, might have stood for the picture of 'Debauch.'

Grinnell's sharp eyes saw Katey as she peeped, but he did not seem to notice. Presently he spoke loudly, so loudly that Katey could hear.

'Now, O'Sullivan, that will freshen you, I hope, and make you think clearly, but I won't give you any more, so don't ask me.'

'What do you mean?' asked Jerry, in amazement, for up to that moment Grinnell had been pressing him to drink.

'Never mind what I mean; only I won't give you any more.'

'Are you jokin'?'

'I am not.'

Jerry looked at him angrily a moment, and then flattening his hat down on his head, said:

'Oh, very well – oh, very well. Then I'll go somewhere else.'

Katey was afraid he would see her, so left the doorway and hurried down the street.

Jerry came home about breakfast-time in a frightfully bad humour. He had had just enough of liquor to make him wish for more, and having tried to get credit several places and been refused, felt a savage disappointment. The sight of Katey's disfigured face in no wise tended to mollify him, and he spoke to her with a harshness that was almost savage:

'Why don't you put somethin' on your face?'

Katey did not know what to say, so remained silent.

'Put somethin' on it, I tell you. Am I to be always made wretched by you?'

Katey could only murmur:

'Always, Jerry? Always?' and began to cry.

'Stop your cryin', I tell you. Here – I'll not stay here any longer. No wonder I have to keep away when I find nothin' here but tears.'

'Jerry, dear, I won't cry,' said Katey, in affright, lest he should go out. 'I won't cry, dear, and I'll cover up my face – only don't go out yet. Look, I am not cryin' now. See, I'm laughin'.'

'Stop your laughin', I say. There isn't much to laugh at here.'

This was too much for Katey, and again she broke down. Jerry got up to go out; she went to the door, and standing before it, said:

'For God's sake, Jerry, don't go out yet.'

'Let me go, I say. Will you dare to stop me.'

'Oh, Jerry, for the sake of the children, don't go out. For the sake of the love you used to have' –

'Out of the way, I say.'

'Oh, Jerry.'

'Let me go, I tell you. You won't. Then take that,' and again he struck her. She cowered away with a low wail. As he left the room, Jerry said, with an effort at self-justification:

'I see the way to manage you, now. Take care that you don't rouse the devil in me.'

Katey was sobbing still when Grinnell came to ask 'how Jerry was this morning.' She felt glad to see him on account of his refusing to give Jerry drink, and shook him warmly by the hand.

Grinnell looked at her without speaking, but manifestly taking notice of her bruised face; then he turned away and seemed as if drying an unostentatious tear. Katey felt drawn towards him by the manifestation of sympathy; and so it was with an open heart that she commenced to thank him for his promise to assist in reclaiming Jerry.

'Don't distress yourself,' he said after some talk, 'you see the influence I have over him, not only personally, but from my position, is ever great. He owes me money' – Katey winced, he noticed it, and kept harping on that string – 'he owes me, I may say, a good deal of money, not that I want him to pay me yet, or that I ever mean to press him for it, but owing me a good deal of money, you know, I can put the screw on him any time I like. For instance, if he did anything to offend me, or if anyone belonging to him got in my way, and I wished it, I could put my thumb on him and crush him like a fly.'

Katey laid her hand on his arm and asked him pleadingly –

'Oh, don't talk like that, it seems so dreadful to me that it frightens me.'

'There, there, my dear,' he answered, patting her shoulder, 'don't fret, I do not mean to crush him like a fly. I only mention it to show you what I could do if I had occasion to. You see when a man is down the hill the best thing for him is to have some determined friend who can crack the whip over his head.'

Katey began to get frightened, she did not know why. She was without knowing from what cause getting a repulsion and fear for the man before her. It might be, she thought, when she asked herself the question, from his hideous aspect, which was enough to alarm anyone. The thought of Jerry being in the power of anyone was a bitter one to her, but that of Jerry being in the power of this man was too dreadful to be realised.

Grinnell, who was watching her closely, saw that some idea of the kind was in her mind, and tried with all his might to banish it. He made kind promises, he offered to do generous acts, he spoke kindly and tenderly to Katey, using every means to rule her reason. But still that instinct which is above all reason spoke in her, and whispered her even not to trust to him. Grinnell saw that he was not making way in her good graces, and took his leave shortly, showing by his manner that he was hurt, though not offended.

Katey was so glad to get rid of him that she was not as kind in her manner as usual. When the door closed behind him she sank with a sigh of relief on one of the two chairs which still remained to them. The children, who had hidden in affright behind the bed as Grinnell had entered, scared by his frightful face, now came forward and hid their little heads in her lap, and began to cuddle her in their pretty way.

After Grinnell had departed, Katey began to take herself to task for not feeling more kindly towards him. The natural justice of her disposition told her that so far as she knew he had acted kindly, and intended to act more kindly still. But then in her heart arose the counterpleading – 'so far as she knew' – and she still continued to mistrust.

Jerry remained out all that day; Katey was almost afraid to go look for him – partly lest she should arouse his anger towards her for following him, and so widen the breach between them, and partly because with womanly delicacy she feared that the sight of her swollen face might tend to lower him amongst his companions.

It was not till the time for closing the public houses came that she ventured in desperation to go in search of him; she tried Grinnell's expecting to find him there. There was no one in the place except the proprietor; and Katey, after some hesitation, pushed open the door and entered. Grinnell, with an exclamation, came from behind the bar, and shook her hand.

'I was just going to call up to see you,' he said.

'What for?'

'To tell you about Jerry.'

'About Jerry? What about him, sir?' asked Katey, in alarm.

'Do not fret yourself, my dear. It will be all right.'

'What will? For God's sake tell me if anything is wrong? Remember he is my husband?'

'Very well, then. He got into trouble to-day. He took too much to drink, and began fighting, and the police got hold of him.'

This was too much for Katey. She fainted.

When she recovered, Grinnell informed her 'that Jerry was in the lock-up, where he would be detained all night, and that he would be brought before the magistrate in the morning.'

Katey never closed an eye that night. The greater part of the time she passed on her knees in prayer, in the rest she watched her children as they slept. In the morning early she was off to the pawnbrokers with some of the last of their goods to raise money to pay Jerry's fine in case one should be imposed. She was at the police-court long before the time of commencing business, and having got into the court waited as patiently as she could till Jerry should be tried.

When business did commence she had still to wait for a good while, for there were a large number of cases to be tried, and as the time when he *must* appear grew closer and closer her heart beat faster and faster till she had to press her hand on her side from pain. At last Jerry's case came on. It was a cruel blow to Katey to see her husband standing in the dock with his head hanging down, and a policeman standing beside him.

The charge, although exactly similar to many that had preceded it, seemed a terrible one to poor Katey, so terrible that she could not see anything but the dire punishment of imprisonment before Jerry, for her wifely fears multiplied everything many fold.

Some witnesses were called, and deposed to such things as fully supported the charge of assault. One of the attorneys who defend criminals in the police-courts spoke in favour of Jerry, and in the course of his remarks mentioned that it was a first offence, and that his client had up to the night before never struck a blow in his life. At this statement the complainant, who was standing by, laughed a loud ironical laugh, suddenly checked as he caught the magistrate's eye fixed on him. The magistrate was a clever man and a very experienced one, and although he said nothing he kept his wits about him. Presently his eye wandered over the court, and he soon fixed on Katey's anxious face. As he noticed the signs of ill-usage a look grew imperceptibly over his face, and the officers of the court who knew his looks felt that it boded ill for Jerry. He allowed the case to spin out a few minutes till he saw Jerry recognise his wife – he knew that she was his wife, and that to him was due her ill-treatment from the flush in his face. Then, when the case was concluded, instead of imposing a fine, as Jerry had anticipated, he ordered him a week's imprisonment with hard labour. It was one of his resolves to put down wife-beating if he could.

Jerry covered his face with his hands: and Katey was just about to rush forward with a wild prayer of mercy on her lips when a policeman standing by pulled her back, saying in a kindly voice:

'No use, my girl. It would only get you into trouble, and could do no good. Best go home and take care of the children till he comes out.'

Katey felt the wisdom of the remark, and stayed still.

Before Jerry left the dock he dropped his hands from his face and looked round the court with a hard cold look of recklessness that made Katey shudder. He did not seem to notice her at first, but seemed to include her in the category of his enemies. As he passed her on his way out, however, he gave her a look which said to her as plainly as if he had used the words –

'This is your work. You couldn't keep your cut face away for once. Very well, you'll see that I'll be even with you yet.'

Katey went home without crying. Despair is dry-eyed when it is most blank. It had seemed to her at each successive disaster that now at last had come the culmination of all that was most dreadful to be borne; but it was not till now that she knew the bitterness of despair. It was not even that Jerry no longer loved her, but that he hated her, and to her attributed a shame that she would have given her life to avert.

Grinnell called to her to try his powers of consolation. He told her most soothingly that a week was not long, and that the shock of the sentence would tend to sober Jerry; and, with many arguments of a like kind, tried to raise her spirits. He stayed a long time, and left her in a tranquil frame of mind.

He came again for a few minutes in the evening, and made some kindly offers of help, which, however, she did not accept.

Next day he came again; and every day that week – sometimes twice in the day. Katey did not like his coming so often, but he seemed so disinterested and kindly-disposed that she did not like to hurt his feelings by telling him so.

At last her eyes were opened to the fact that instinct may be stronger than reason.

She was working in the theatre, where she had got a job of cleaning to do, when she overheard some of the men talking. Katey was too honourable to voluntarily listen, and would never have done so in cold blood, but she heard her husband's name mentioned, and the curiosity arising from her great love, which made her anxious to find how he stood in the opinions of his companions, made her pause and listen with bated breath.

She found what pained her much, and yet had in it a gleam of hope. The men seemed to think that Jerry was drifting into being a hopeless drunkard, and that if he continued to go on, as he had been going on, he would get an attack of delirium tremens. One of them remarked presently:

'That was a damnable trick of Grin's.'

'What was that?' asked another.

'Don't you know? or you? or you? Why, men, you're as blind as bats. *I* saw it all long ago.'

'Saw what? Out with it, man.'

'Well, you see, Grinnell is sweet on the pretty little Irish-woman, and wanted to get the husband out of the way – What's that?'

It was the stir Katey made as she rose from her knees, where she had been scrubbing and leaned against the wall, with her heart beating wildly and her face on fire.

'Well, but what was the trick?'

'Why, man, can't you see? He put Dirty Dick up to make him pick a quarrel when he was full of drink, and then quietly sent the pot-boy to send round a policeman.'

'Oh, the blackguard. Tell you what, boys, we oughtn't to stand that,' the voice was that of a man who had not yet spoken.

'Don't make a blamed ass of yourself. What call is it of ours? Don't you see that it would do no good. The woman is glad enough of it for all she takes on.'

'How do you know that?'

'How do I know it? Why, because I have eyes, and ears, and amn't a fool. Sure he spends half the day with her, till all the neighbours are beginnin' to talk.'

Katey felt as though she were going mad. The scales seemed to have fallen from her eyes, and, with the clear light of her present knowledge, she understood the villainy of Grinnell. She was afraid to hear more, and moved away and worked with such desperation, that presently her strength began to leave her.

When her work over she tottered home, being scarcely able to walk steadily, and having arrived, shut the door behind her and locked it; and then she lay down on her bed in a state of mental and physical prostration, which was akin to death.

When Grinnell called he found the door locked, and, having knocked several times without getting any answer, went away without saying a word.

10

The End of the Journey

Katey waited in, in the morning, at the time at which Grinnell had been in the habit of calling for the last few days; her object was to avoid him, and she feared meeting him if she should go out. Later on, however, when she had to go to her work, she met him outside the door of the house, where he had evidently been waiting for some time. She pretended not to see him, and walked quickly down the street. He walked alongside of her in silence for a while before he spoke.

'What's the meaning of all this?'

Katey hurried still faster, dragging her poor shawl closer as she went.

After another pause, Grinnell said again:

'You seem to have changed?'

'I have.' She turned, as she spoke, and looked him full in the face.

Something told him that her mind was made up, and that she knew or suspected his villainy; and there was passion in his voice now.

'It was mighty quick.'

'It was.'

After a pause he said, so slowly and impressively, and with such hidden purpose, that she grew cold as she listened:

'People are often too quick; it would sometimes be better for them – and those belonging to them – if they were a little slower.'

Seeing that she did not answer he changed his tone.

'A man can put his thumb on a fly – I wonder have flies wives – or children?' He said the last words with a tone of deadly malice.

Katey winced, but said nothing. Grinnell saw that he was

foiled, and all the hate of his nature spoke. He came closer to Katey and hissed at her:

'Take care! I am not to be got rid of so easily as you think. I will be revenged on you for your scorn, bitterly revenged; and even when I see you crawling in the dust at my feet, I shall spurn you. Wait till you see your husband a hopeless drunkard, and your children in the workhouse burial-cart, and then perhaps you will be sorry that you despised me.'

Still seeing no signs of any answer, he added:

'Very well. It's war – is it then? Good-bye to you,' and, so saying, he turned on his heel and left her.

Katey worked all that day as if in a dream, and when her work was over, shut herself up again with her children. The next day was the same. She did not see Grinnell, but somehow she mistrusted his silence even more than she feared his malice.

When the time came for Jerry's liberation, Katey was in waiting outside the prison door. Katey had made herself look as smart as possible, and the bruises on her face were nearly well. When Jerry caught sight of her, he started as if with a glad surprise, but the instant after, as if from remembrance, a dark frown gathered on his face, and he walked past her without seeming to notice her present. Katey was cut to the heart, but, nevertheless, she did not let her pain appear on her face. She came and touched him on the shoulder and said:

'Jerry, dear, here I am.'

'I see you' – this in a harsh, cold voice.

'Are you coming home, dear.'

'Ay, a nice home.'

'Come home, Jerry.'

'I will not. I must get something to make my hair grow,' and without another word he strode away from her side. She went home and wept bitterly.

Jerry came home drunk late that night, and neither then nor the next morning would speak kindly to his wife. In the afternoon he went to the theatre, but found that his place had been given away.

He could get no work that suited him, and after a few days' seeking, gave it up as a hopeless task, and took to drinking all day long in Grinnell's, where he was allowed credit.

As he earned no money, the entire support of the family once more devolved on Katey, and once again the brave little woman tried to meet the storm. Morning, noon, and night she worked, when work could be got; but the long suffering and anxiety had told on her strength, and, in addition, there had lately come a new trial. Mrs O'Sullivan had got a stroke of paralysis, and her failing business had entirely deserted her. She now required help, and as Jerry could give none, had been removed to the workhouse.

Day after day things got worse and worse. The room, up to the present occupied, had to be given up as Katey could not pay for it, and the change was to a squalid garret, bare, and bleak, and cold. One by one the last necessary articles of furniture vanished, till nothing was left but an old table and chair, and some wretched bed gear, which had not been worth pawning, and which now covered two wretched beds, knocked up by Jerry with old boards. Jerry, too, had gone down and down. He was not the scoff of his comrades, for he was too quarrelsome, but he was their unconscious tool, and occupied a position somewhat akin to that of a vicious bull-dog ready to be set at any comer. Grinnell gave him as much drink as he required, and in every way tried to get him into his power.

Jerry often struck his wife now, and it was not due to his efforts that he did not do it oftener. When he was drunk she always kept as much as possible out of the way, often waiting outside the door till he had fallen asleep, well knowing that if he met her she would suffer violence. More than once he was arrested either for drunkenness or assault, or both, and so often that his hair never had time to grow to a decent length.

After this life had gone on for some time, and Katey was showing signs of failing health, Grinnell tried to renew his acquaintance. Katey told him plainly that she would have nothing to do with him in any way, not even so far as speaking to him was concerned. He answered with such a cruel threat that Katey fainted. This was in the street, and whilst she was still senseless a policeman appeared, sent by Grinnell, who had told him that there was a drunken woman lying on the pathway.

The man, with the instinct of his profession, which sees a crime in every doubtful case, procured assistance, and brought her to the station-house, which was close at hand. There she was restored with a little care, but the charge of drunkenness had been preferred against her, and she would not be allowed to go home. The sergeant in charge said that he would allow her to go home if she got bail. She did not know where to turn to; she could only sit down in the cell and cry. Presently Grinnell, who knew what would happen, arrived, and having ascertained the state of the case went through the formality of going bail, and Katey was released. Grinnell was waiting outside, and walked up the street with her. Katey walked so fast that he had trouble to keep up with her.

'I think you might speak to me after I have kept you out of jail?' Katey did not answer. He waited, and then said, 'Very well, go your own road. If anything happens to you just think of me.' Then he walked away.

Katey did not sleep that night. She knew that on the morrow she would have to stand in the dock charged with an offence whose very name she hated; and she did not know where in the wide world to look for help in case a fine should be imposed. She could not look into the possibility of her being sent to prison. It was too terrible both for herself and her children.

Early in the morning she rose. Jerry had not been home all night, and so she had been unable to tell him of the charge.

There was still one article in the room on which money could be raised. This was Jerry's tool-basket, which, with something of traditional reverence and something of hope, he had still spared. He could not bear to pledge the tools he had worked with, and both he and Katey felt that whilst these tools remained to his hand there was a prospect that things would mend. Katey now regarded the tool-basket with longing eyes. She felt that should she be sent to prison there was hunger and suffering and, perhaps, ruin for her children, and a shame that would make Jerry worse. She thought of pledging it, but the thought arose to restrain her – 'It would take away Jerry's last hope – pull down the prop of his better life, and his wife's should not be the hand to do this at any cost.' And so she spared the basket.

She had to wait a long time in the court, and when she was put in the dock felt faintish. However, she nerved herself, and answered all the questions put to her. The magistrate was a kind and just one, and recognised truth in her story, and ordered her to be discharged. She left the court crying, after calling down a thousand blessings on his head.

When she came home she found the basket gone. Jerry had taken it that very morning and pledged it to get money for dissipation. This was a great blow to Katey, for she felt that despair was gathering when Jerry had made up his mind to part with his tools. Nevertheless, she felt in her heart a gleam of comfort in the thought that she had acted rightly, and that the prop had not been shorn away by her hand.

Jerry drank frightfully that day, and came home early in the evening in a state of semi-madness. He rushed into the room and caught Katey by the shoulder so roughly that she screamed out. He said hoarsely –

'Is this true what I heard about you?'

'What, Jerry? Oh, let go of me, you are hurting me.'

'What? I suppose you don't know. Well, I'll tell you – that you were run in for bein' drunk?'

'Let me explain, Jerry dear.'

'Let me explain, Jerry dear. Explain away, but you won't explain that out of my head. So this is my model wife that abuses me for gettin' drunk. This is the woman that thinks it wrong and a sin. I know you now.'

Katey spoke in desperation –

'Jerry, listen to me. I was not drunk. I fainted in the street, and they brought me to the station, but indeed, indeed I was not drunk. I haven't tasted even a drop of liquor for years – sure don't you believe me, Jerry. I was discharged this morning. The magistrate said there was no case against me.'

'Ay, fine talk that. But I've heard about it already. Grinnell told me all about it.'

'Grinnell told you! Oh, Jerry, take care what that man tells you of me.'

'What do you mean?'

The question was asked in a tone of bitter suspicion.

'I mean that that wicked, wicked man hates me, and would do me harm if he could.'

'What do you mean I say? Why does he hate you? Why should he hate you?'

Jerry was now so violent that Katey was afraid to tell him lest he should do something desperate. Jerry grew more and more violent, and finally struck her severely in the bosom with his clenched fist, and ran out swearing horribly.

When he came home that night Katey searched in his pocket and found the pawn ticket for his tools. The sum was only for a few shillings, and she resolved that if she possibly could she would redeem them, and then go herself and look for some work for him.

Accordingly, next day she went out and pledged the only thing left to her worth pledging – her wedding ring. It cost her many an effort, and many a bitter tear, but for too long bitterness had been her fortune to be deterred from action by it now. She got back the tool basket, and left it on the table where Jerry would see it when he returned.

So she waited and waited all though the long day.

Jerry was drinking at Grinnell's, and was in such a state of despondency that his liquor seemed to have hardly any effect on him. Grinnell supplied him freely, for he had a design of vengeance against Katey on hands, and desired to work Jerry, whom he had fixed on as his tool, to the required pitch. Mons was present, too, and Sebright, and Popham, and Dirty Dick, who had been primed up to do Grinnell's bidding.

By and by Jerry began to be excited, and grew quarrelsome. Dirty Dick, at a sign from Grinnell, put himself in his way, and an altercation arose. Jerry had a spite against the latter as being the means of his being put in gaol for the first time, and commenced hostilities at once.

'Get out, you dog. You want to fight, I suppose. Best mind out or I'll give you what I gave you before.'

'You had better. Who laughed at the wrong side of his mouth after that? Who got his hair cut – eh? Look, boys, it hasn't grown since.'

Jerry began to get savage.

'Here, get out, I've murder in me.'

Grinnell, as he heard the latter remark, smiled softly to himself – a smile that boded no good to poor Katey. Dirty Dick ran behind Popham and peered over his shoulder in mock fear.

'Don't stir, man, don't you see I'm goin' to be murdered by the long-haired man?'

Jerry was getting furious, but they still continued to irritate him. Dirty Dick said again –

'How is your wife, Irishman? Have you been beating her lately, or has she been run in for being drunk?'

This was too much for Jerry. By a sudden rush he caught the man by the throat, and before he could be torn away from him had inflicted some desperate blows, one of which laid his cheek open.

Then Dick lost his temper in turn and spoke out again, this time without heeding what he said, for he merely meant to wound.

'Better go home and look after your wife.'

'What does he mean?' asked Jerry.

'I mean what I mean. Ask Grinnell?'

The individual named seemed to grow paler. He saw that his tool was reckless and feared for himself – both personally from Jerry's violence, should he find out his treachery, and in his character if such things should be known by the frequenters of his house. He came from behind the bar and laid his hand on Dick's shoulder.

Dirty Dick shook him off. 'Let me alone,' he said.

Grinnell whispered to him –

'Hush, man, do you know what you are saying? Best keep your temper or I'll put my thumb on you.'

'Damn your thumb. Don't threaten me. I'm reckless now.'

Grinnell saw that another row was the only way to check his tongue, and struck him. The two men were at once seized and held, and then Dick gave his tongue full play. He spoke of Katey so foully that the men cried shame on him. He told Jerry how all the neighbours were talking of her and Grinnell. How Grinnell had paid him to get up a fight, so that he might be put in gaol and leave the field clear. He spoke with such an air of truth, and all he said being true, except his foul speeches about Katey, fitted so well into

Jerry's knowledge of things, that he took it all as true. There is no lie so damaging as that which is partly true. The shock of hearing all these things and believing them sobered Jerry, and he grew calm. Seeing him so the men let him go, and having done so did not attempt to lay hands on him, for there was a look in his face so deadly, that they were afraid. He said no word; he looked at no one but Grinnell, and at him only one glance, which said, 'Wait' so plainly, that Grinnell shuddered. Then he walked out of the room, and there was silence.

Jerry walked home on set purpose, and entered the garret where Katey, wearied out of her long waiting, lay asleep in bed. The first things he saw was the tool basket on the table, beside a bottle and glass. He pulled off his coat and flung it on the table, and hurled the basket on to the floor. Katey woke with the noise, and the children woke also, and sat up with their little eyes fixed with terror. Jerry went to the bedside and caught Katey's hand. 'Get up,' he said. Katey was rising, when he pulled her impatiently out on the floor, bringing down the bed also.

Katey rose and stood before him. She saw that something dreadful was the matter, and thought that he had got into more fresh trouble. She said to him lovingly, 'Oh, Jerry, if there is trouble, sure I am here to share it with you. Jerry – we will begin fresh to-morrow. Look, dear, I have got back your tools.'

'How did you get them? Where did the money come from?'

'Don't ask me, Jerry.'

'Where did the money come from – answer me at once, or' – He spoke so savagely that she grew cold.

'Jerry, I sold my wedding ring.'

Jerry laughed – the hard, cold laugh of a demon. 'Time for you to sell it.'

She saw that there was some hidden meaning in his words, and asked him what he meant. 'I mean that when you have a husband in every man, you need no ring.'

'For shame, Jerry, for shame. What have I done to deserve all this?'

Jerry grew furious. The big veins stood out on his forehead and his eyes rolled.

THE MURDER OF KATEY

'Done!' he said. 'Done! What about Grinnell?'

Then without another word, or if the very idea was too much for him, he stooped and picked up a hammer which had rolled out of the tool-basket.

Katey saw the act and screamed, for she read murder in his eyes. He clutched her by the arm and raised the hammer; she struggled wildly, but he shook her off, and then, with a glare like that of a wild beast, struck her on the temple.

She fell as if struck by lightning.

When he saw her lying on the floor, with the blood streaming round her and forming a pool, the hammer dropped from his hand, and he stood as one struck blind.

So he stood a moment, then knelt beside her and tried to coax her back to life.

'Katey, Katey, what have I done? Oh, God, what have I done? I have murdered her. Oh? the drink! the drink! Why didn't I stay at home and this wouldn't have happened?'

He stopped suddenly, and, rushing over to the tool-basket, took up a chisel, and with one fierce motion drew it across his throat, and fell down beside the body of his wife.

Buried Treasures

1

The Old Wreck

Mr Stedman spoke.

'I do not wish to be too hard on you; but I will not, I cannot consent to Ellen's marrying you till you have sufficient means to keep her in comfort. I know too well what poverty is. I saw her poor mother droop and pine away till she died, and all from poverty. No, no, Ellen must be spared that sorrow at all events.'

'But, sir, we are young. You say you have always earned your living. I can do the same and I thought' – this with a flush – 'I thought that if I might be so happy as to win Ellen's love that you might help us.'

'And so I would, my dear boy; but what help could I give? I find it hard to keep the pot boiling as it is, and there is only Ellen and myself to feed. No, no, I must have some certainty for Ellen before I let her leave me. Just suppose anything should happen to me' –

'Then, sir, what could be better than to have some one to look after Ellen – some one with a heart to love her as she should be loved, and a pair of hands to be worked to the bone for her sake.'

'True, boy; true. But still it cannot be. I must be certain of Ellen's future before I trust her out of my own care. Come now, let me see you with a hundred pounds of your own, and I shall not refuse to let you speak to her. But mind, I shall trust to your honour not to forestall that time.'

'It is cruel, sir, although you mean it in kindness. I could as easily learn to fly as raise a hundred pounds with my present opportunities. Just think of my circumstances, sir. If my poor father had lived all would have been different; but you know that sad story.'

'No, I do not. Tell it to me.'

" 'TIS AN ILL WIND THAT BLOWS NO ONE GOOD."

'He left the Gold Coast after spending half his life there toiling for my poor mother and me. We knew from his letter that he was about to start for home, and that he was coming in a small sailing vessel, taking all his savings with him. But from that time to this he has never been heard of.'

'Did you make inquiries?'

'We tried every means, or rather poor mother did, for I was too young, and we could find out nothing.'

'Poor boy. From my heart I pity you; still I cannot change my opinion. I have always hoped that Ellen would marry happily. I have worked for her, early and late, since she was born, and it would be mistaken kindness to let her marry without sufficient provision for her welfare.'

Robert Hamilton left Mr Stedman's cottage in great dejection. He had entered it with much misgiving, but with a hope so strong that it brightened the prospect of success. He went slowly along the streets till he got to his office, and when once there he had so much work to do that little time was left him for reflection until his work for the day was over. That night he lay awake, trying with all the intentness of his nature to conceive some plan by which he might make the necessary sum to entitle him to seek the hand of Ellen Stedman: but all in vain. Scheme after scheme rose up before him, but each one, though born of hope, quickly perished in succession. Gradually his imagination grew in force as the real world seemed to fade away; he built bright castles in the air and installed Ellen as their queen. He thought of all the vast sums of money made each year by chances, of old treasures found after centuries, new treasures dug from mines, and turned from mills and commerce. But all these required capital – except the old treasures – and this source of wealth being a possibility, to it his thoughts clung as a man lost in mid-ocean clings to a spar – clung as he often conceived that his poor father had clung when lost with all his treasure far at sea.

'Vigo Bay, the Schelde, already giving up their long-buried spoil,' so thought he. 'All round our coasts lie millions lost, hidden but for a time. Other men have benefited by them – why should not I have a chance also?' And then, as he sunk to sleep the possibility seemed to become reality, and as he slept he found treasure after treasure, and all was real to him, for he knew not that he dreamt.

He had many dreams. Most of them connected with the finding of treasures, and in all of them Ellen took a prominent place. He seemed in his dreams to renew his first acquaintance with the girl he loved, and when he thought of the accident that brought them together, it might be expected that the seashore was the scene of many of his dreams. The meeting was in this wise: One holiday, some three years before, he had been walking on the flat shore of the 'Bull,' when he noticed at some distance off a very beautiful young girl, and set to longing for some means of making her acquaintance. The means came even as he wished. The wind was blowing freely, and the girl's hat blew off and hurried seawards over the flat shore. He ran after it and brought it back: and from that hour the two had, after their casual acquaintance had been sanctioned by her father, became fast friends.

Most of his dreams of the night had faded against morning, but one he remembered.

He seemed to be in a wide stretch of sand near the hulk of a great vessel. Beside him lay a large iron-bound box of great weight, which he tried in vain to lift. He had by a lever just forced it through a hole in the side of the ship, and it had fallen on the sand and was sinking. Despite all he could do, it still continued to go down into the sand, but by slow degrees. The mist was getting round him, shutting out the moonlight, and from far he could hear a dull echoing roar muffled by the fog, and the air seemed laden with the clang of distant bells. Then the air became instinct with the forms of life, and amid them floated the form of Ellen, and with her presence the gloom and fog and darkness were dispelled, and the sun rose brightly on the instant, and all was fair and happy.

Next day was Sunday, and so after prayers he went for a walk with his friend, Tom Harrison.

They directed their steps towards Dollymount, and passing across the bridge, over Crab Lake, found themselves on the North Bull. The tide was 'black' out, and when they crossed the line of low bent-covered sand-hills, or dunnes as they are called in Holland, a wide stretch of sand intersected with shallow tidal streams lay before them, out towards the mouth of the bay. As they looked, Robert's dream of the night before flashed into his memory, and he expected to see before him the hulk of the old ship.

Presently Tom remarked:

'I do not think I ever saw the tide so far out before. What an immense stretch of sand there is. It is a wonder there is no rock or anything of the kind all along this shore.'

'There is one,' said Robert, pointing to where, on the very edge of the water, rose a little mound, seemingly a couple of feet at most, over the level of the sand.

'Let us go out to it,' said Tom, and accordingly they both took off their boots and stockings, and walked over the wet sand, and forded the shallow streams till they got within a hundred yards of the mound. Suddenly Tom called out: 'It is not a rock at all; it is a ship, bottom upwards, with the end towards us, and sunk in the sand.'

Robert's heart stood still for an instant.

What if this should be a treasure-ship, and his dream prove prophetic? In an instant more he shook aside the fancy and hurried on.

They found that Tom had not been mistaken. There lay the hulk of an old ship, with just its bottom over the sand. Close round it the ebb and flow of the tide had worn a hole like the moat round an old castle; and in this pool small fishes darted about, and lazy crabs sidled into the sand.

Tom jumped the narrow moat, and stood balanced on the keel, and a hard task he had to keep his footing on the slippery seaweed. He tapped the timbers with his stick, and they gave back a hollow sound. 'The inside is not yet choked up,' he remarked.

Robert joined him, and walked all over the bottom of the ship, noticing how some of the planks, half rotten with long exposure, were sinking inwards.

After a few minutes Tom spoke –

'I say, Bob, suppose that this old ship was full of money, and that you and I could get it out.'

'I have just been thinking the same.'

'Suppose we try,' said Tom, and he commenced to endeavour to prize up the end of a broken timber with his stick. Robert watched him for some minutes, and when he had given up the attempt in despair, spoke –

'Suppose we do try, Tom. I have a very strange idea. I had a curious dream last night, and this old ship reminds me of it.'

Tom asked Robert to tell the dream. He did so, and when he had finished, and had also confided his difficulty about the hundred pounds, Tom remarked –

'We'll try the hulk, at any rate. Let us come some night and cut a hole in her and look. It might be worth our while; it will be a lark at any rate.'

He seemed so interested in the matter that Robert asked him the reason.

'Well, I will tell you,' he said. 'You know Tomlinson. Well, he told me the other day that he was going to ask Miss Stedman to marry him. He is well off – comparatively, and unless you get your chance soon you may be too late. Don't be offended at me for telling you. I wanted to get an opportunity.'

'Thanks, old boy,' was Robert's answer, as he squeezed his hand. No more was spoken for a time. Both men examined the hulk carefully, and then came away, and sat again on a sand hill.

Presently a coastguard came along, with his telescope under his arm. Tom entered into conversation with him about the wreck.

'Well, sir,' he said, 'that was afore my time here. I've been here only about a year, and that's there a matter o' fifteen year or thereabouts. She came ashore here in the great storm when the "Mallard" was lost in the Scillies. I've heerd tell' –

Robert interrupted him to ask –

'Did anyone ever try what was in her?'

'Well, sir, there I'm out. By rights there should, but I've bin told that about then there was a lawsuit on as to who the shore belonged to. The ship lay in the line between the Ballast Board ground and the Manor ground, or whatever it is, and so nothin' could be done till the suit was ended, and when it was there weren't much use lookin' for anything, for

she was settled nigh as low as she is now, and if there ever
was anything worth havin' in her the salt water had ruined
it long ago.

'Then she was never examined?' said Tom.

'Most like not, sir; they don't never examine little ships
like her – if she was a big one we might,' and the coastguard
departed.

When he was gone Tom said, 'By Jove, he forgot to say on
whose ground she is,' and he ran after him to ask the question. When he came back he said, 'It's all right; it belongs to
Sir Arthur Forres.'

After watching for some time in silence Robert said, 'Tom,
I have very strange thoughts about this. Let us get leave
from Sir Arthur – he is, I believe, a very generous man – and
regularly explore.'

'Done,' said Tom, and, it being now late, they returned to
town.

2

Wind and Tide

Robert and Tom next day wrote a letter to Sir Arthur Forres asking him to let them explore the ship, and by return of post got a kind answer, not only granting the required permission, but making over the whole ship to them to do what they pleased with. Accordingly they held a consultation as to the best means of proceeding, and agreed to commence operations as soon as possible, as it was now well on in December, and every advance of winter would throw new obstacles in their way. Next day they bought some tools, and brought them home in great glee. It often occurred to both of them that they were setting out on the wildest of wild-goose chases, but the novelty and excitement of the whole affair always overcame their scruples. The first moonlight night that came they took their tools, and sallied out to Dollymount to make the first effort on their treasure ship. So intent were they on their object that their immediate surroundings did not excite their attention. It was not, therefore, till they arrived at the summit of the sand hill, from which they had first seen the hulk, that they discovered that the tide was coming in, and had advanced about half way. The knowledge was like a cold bath to each of them, for here were all their hopes dashed to the ground, for an indefinite time at least. It might be far into the winter time – perhaps months – before they could get a union of tide, moonlight, and fair weather, such as alone could make their scheme practicable. They had already tried to get leave from office, but so great was the press of business that their employer told them that unless they had special business, which they could name, he could not dispense with their services. To name their object would be to excite ridicule, and as the whole affair was but based on a chimera they were of course silent.

They went home sadder than they had left it, and next day, by a careful study of the almanac, made out a list of the nights which might suit their purpose – if moon and weather proved favourable. From the fact of their living in their employer's house their time was further curtailed, for it was an inflexible rule that by twelve o'clock everyone should be home. Therefore, the only nights which could suit were those from the 11th to the 15th December, on which there would be low water between the hours of seven and eleven. This would give them on each night about one hour in which to work, for that length of time only was the wreck exposed between the ebbing and flowing tides.

They waited in anxiety for the 11th December, the weather continued beautifully fine, and nearly every night the two friends walked to view the scene of their future operations. Robert was debarred from visiting Ellen by her father's direction, and so was glad to have some object of interest to occupy his thoughts whilst away from her.

As the time wore on, the weather began to change, and Robert and Tom grew anxious. The wind began to blow in short sharp gusts, which whirled the sodden dead leaves angrily about exposed corners, and on the seaboard sent the waves shorewards topped with angry crests. Misty clouds came drifting hurriedly over the sea, and at times the fog became so thick that it was hardly possible to see more than a few yards ahead, still the young men continued to visit their treasure every night. At first, the coastguards had a watchful eye on them, noticing which they unfolded their purpose and showed Sir Arthur's letter making the ship over to their hands.

The sailors treated the whole affair as a good joke, but still promised to do what they could to help them, in the good-humoured way which is their special charm. A certain fear had for some time haunted the two friends – a fear which neither of them had ever spoken out. From brooding so much as they did on their adventure, they came to think, or rather to feel, that the ship which for fifteen years had been unnoticed and untouched in the sand, had suddenly acquired as great an interest in the eyes of all the world as of themselves. Accordingly, they thought that some evil-designing person might try to cut them out of their adventure by forestalling them in searching the wreck. Their fear was dispelled by the kindly promise of the coastguards not to let anyone meddle with the vessel without their permission. As the weather continued to get more and more broken, the very disappointment of their hopes, which the break threatened served to enlarge those hopes, and when on the night of the tenth they heard a wild storm howling round the chimneys, as they lay in bed, each was assured in his secret heart that the old wreck contained such a treasure as the world had seldom seen.

Seven o'clock next night saw them on the shore of the Bull looking out into the pitchy darkness. The wind was blowing so strongly inshore that the waves were driven high beyond their accustomed line at the same state of the tide, and the channels were running like mill-dams. As each wave came down over the flat shore it was broke up into a mass of foam and spray, and the wind swept away the spume until on shore it fell like rain. Far along the sandy shore was heard the roaring of the waves, hoarsely bellowing, so that hearing the sound we could well imagine how the district got its quaint name.

On such a night it would have been impossible to have worked at the wreck, even could the treasure-seekers have reached it, or could they have even found it in the pitchy darkness. They waited some time, but seeing that it was in vain, they sadly departed homeward, hoping fondly that the next evening would prove more propitious.

Vain were their hopes. The storm continued for two whole days, for not one moment of which, except between the pauses of the rushing or receding waves, was the wreck exposed. Seven o'clock each night saw the two young men looking over the sand-hills, waiting in the vain hope of a chance of visiting the vessel, hoping against hope that a sudden calm would give the opportunity they wished. When the storm began to abate their hopes were proportionally raised, and on the morning of the 14th when they awoke and could not hear the wind whistling through the chimneys next their attic, they grew again sanguine of success. That night they went to the Bull in hope, and came home filled with despair. Although the storm had ceased, the sea was still rough. Great, heavy, sullen waves, sprayless, but crested ominously, from ridges of foam, came rolling into the bay, swelling onward with great speed and resistless force, and bursting over the shallow waste of sand so violently that even any attempt to reach the wreck was out of the question. As Robert and Tom hurried homeward – they had waited to the latest moment on the Bull, and feared being late – they felt spiritless and dejected. But one more evening remained on which they might possibly visit the wreck, and they feared that even should wind and tide be suitable one hour would not do to explore it. However, youth is never without hope, and next morning they both had that sanguine feeling which is the outcome of despair – the feeling that the tide of fortune must sometime turn, and that the loser as well as the winner has his time. As they neared the Bull that night their hearts beat so loud that they could almost hear them. They felt that there was ground for hope. All the way from town they could see the great flats opposite Clontarf lying black in the moonlight, and they thought that over the sands the same calm must surely rest. But, alas, they did not allow for the fact that two great breakwaters protect the harbour, but that the sands of the Bull are open to all the storms that blow – that the great Atlantic billows, broken up on the northern and southern coasts, yet still strong enough to be feared, sweep up and down the Channel, and beat with every tide into the harbours and bays along the coast. Accordingly, on reaching the sand-hills, they saw what dashed their hopes at once.

The moon rose straight before them beyond the Bailey Lighthouse, and the broad belt of light which stretched from it passed over the treasure-ship. The waves, now black, save where the light caught the sloping sides, lay blank, but ever and anon as they passed on far over their usual range, the black hull rose among the gleams of light. There was not a chance that the wreck could be attempted, and so they went sadly home – remembering the fact that the night of the 24th December was the earliest time at which they could again renew their effort.

3

The Iron Chest

The days that intervened were long to both men.

To Robert they were endless; even the nepenthe* of continued hard work could not quiet his mind. Distracted on one side by his forbidden love for Ellen, and on the other by the expected fortune by which he might win her, he could hardly sleep at night. When he did sleep he always dreamed, and in his dreams Ellen and the wreck were always associated. At one time his dream would be of unqualified good fortune – a vast treasure found and shared with his love; at another, all would be gloom, and in the search for the treasure he would endanger his life, or, what was far greater pain, forfeit her love.

However, it is one consolation, that, whatever else may happen in the world, time wears on without ceasing, and the day longest expected comes at last.

On the evening of the 24th December, Tom and Robert took their way to Dollymount in breathless excitement.

As they passed through town, and saw the vast concourse of people all intent on one common object – the preparation for the greatest of all Christian festivals – the greatest festival, which is kept all over the world, wherever the True Light has fallen, they could not but feel a certain regret that they, too, could not join in the throng. Robert's temper was somewhat ruffled by seeing Ellen leaning on the arm of Tomlinson, looking into a brilliantly-lighted shop window, so intently, that she did not notice him passing. When they had left the town, and the crowds, and the overflowing stalls, and brilliant holly-decked shops, they did not so much mind, but hurried on.

---

* nepenthe – a drink or drug to alleviate sorrow.

CHRISTMAS EVE

So long as they were within city bounds, and even whilst there were brightly-lit shop windows, all seemed light enough. When, however, they were so far from town as to lose the glamour of the lamplight in the sky overhead, they began to fear that the night would indeed be too dark for work.

They were prepared for such an emergency, and when they stood on the slope of sand, below the dunnes, they lit a dark lantern and prepared to cross the sands. After a few moments they found that the lantern was a mistake. They saw the ground immediately before them so far as the sharp triangle of light, whose apex was the bulls-eye, extended, but beyond this the darkness rose like a solid black wall. They closed the lantern, but this was even worse, for after leaving the light, small though it was, their eyes were useless in the complete darkness. It took them nearly an hour to reach the wreck.

At last they got to work, and with hammer and chisel and saw commenced to open the treasure ship.

The want of light told sorely against them, and their work progressed slowly despite their exertions. All things have an end, however, and in time they had removed several planks so as to form a hole some four feet wide, by six long – one of the timbers crossed this; but as it was not in the middle, and left a hole large enough to descend by, it did not matter.

It was with beating hearts that the two young men slanted the lantern so as to turn the light in through the aperture. All within was black, and not four feet below them was a calm glassy pool of water that seemed like ink. Even as they looked this began slowly to rise, and they saw that the tide had turned, and that but a few minutes more remained. They reached down as far as they could, plunging their arms up to their shoulders in the water, but could find nothing. Robert stood up and began to undress.

'What are you going to do?' said Tom.

'Going to dive – it is the only chance we have.'

Tom did not hinder him, but got the piece of rope they had brought with them and fastened it under Robert's shoulders and grasped the other end firmly. Robert arranged the lamp so as to throw the light as much downwards as possi-

ble, and then, with a silent prayer, let himself down through
the aperture and hung on by the beam. The water was
deadly cold – so cold, that, despite the fever heat to which he
was brought through excitement, he felt chilled. Nevertheless he did not hesitate, but, letting go the beam, dropped
into the black water.

'For Ellen,' he said, as he disappeared.

In a quarter of a minute he appeared again, gasping, and
with a convulsive effort climbed the short rope, and stood
beside his friend.

'Well?' asked Tom, excitedly.

'Oh-h-h-h! good heavens, I am chilled to the heart. I went
down about six feet, and then touched a hard substance. I
felt round it, and so far as I can tell it is a barrel. Next to it
was a square corner of a box, and further still something
square made of iron.'

'How do you know it is iron?'

'By the rust. Hold the rope again, there is no time to lose;
the tide is rising every minute, and we will soon have to go.'

Again he went into the black water and this time stayed
longer. Tom began to be frightened at the delay, and shook
the rope for him to ascend. The instant after he appeared
with face almost black with suffused blood. Tom hauled at
the rope, and once more he stood on the bottom of the vessel.
This time he did not complain of the cold. He seemed quiv-
ering with a great excitement that overcame the cold. When
he had recovered his breath he almost shouted out –

'There's something there. I know it – I feel it.'

'Anything strange?' asked Tom, in fierce excitement.

'Yes, the iron box is heavy – so heavy that I could not stir
it. I could easily lift the end of the cask, and two or three
other boxes, but I could not stir it.'

Whilst he was speaking, both heard a queer kind of hiss-
ing noise, and looking down in alarm saw the water running
into the pool around the vessel. A few minutes more and they
would be cut off from shore by some of the tidal streams.
Tom cried out:

'Quick, quick! or we shall be late. We must put down the
beams before the tide rises or it will wash the hold full of
sand.'

Without waiting even to dress, Robert assisted him and they placed the planks on their original position and secured them with a few strong nails. Then they rushed away for shore. When they had reached the sand-hill, Robert, despite his exertions, was so chilled that he was unable to put on his clothes.

To bathe and stay naked for half an hour on a December night is no joke.

Tom drew his clothes on him as well as he could, and after adding his overcoat and giving him a pull from the flask, he was something better. They hurried away, and what with exercise, excitement, and hope were glowing when they reached home.

Before going to bed they held a consultation as to what was best to be done. Both wished to renew their attempt as they could begin at half-past seven o'clock; for although the morrow was Christmas Day, they knew that any attempt to rescue goods from the wreck should be made at once. There were now two dangers to be avoided – rough weather and the drifting of the sand – and so they decided that not a moment was to be lost.

At the daybreak they were up, and the first moment that saw the wreck approachable found them wading out towards it. This time they were prepared for wet and cold. They had left their clothes on the beach and put on old ones, which, even if wet, would still keep off the wind, for a strong, fitful breeze was now blowing in eddies, and the waves were beginning to rise ominously. With beating hearts they examined the closed-up gap; and, as they looked, their hopes fell. One of the timbers had been lifted off by the tide, and from the deposit of sand in the crevices, they feared that much must have found its way in. They had brought several strong pieces of rope with them, for their effort to-day was to be to lift out the iron chest, which both fancied contained a treasure.

Robert prepared himself to descend again. He tied one rope round his waist, as before, and took the other in his hands. Tom waited breathlessly till he returned. He was a long time coming up, and rose with his teeth chattering, but had the rope no longer with him. He told Tom that he had succeeded in putting it under the chest. Then he went down again with the other rope, and when he rose the second time, said that he had put it under also, but crossing the first. He was so chilled that he was unable to go down a third time. Indeed, he was hardly able to stand so cold did he seem; and it was with much shrinking of spirit that his friend prepared to descend to make the ropes fast, for he knew that should anything happen to him Robert could not help him up. This did not lighten his task or serve to cheer his spirits as he went down for the first time into the black water. He took two pieces of rope; his intention being to tie Robert's ropes round the chest, and then bring the spare ends up. When he rose he told Robert that he had tied one of the ropes round the box, but had not time to tie the others. He was so chilled that he could not venture to go down again, and so both men hurriedly closed the gap as well as they could, and went on shore to change their clothes. When they had dressed, and got tolerably warm, the tide had begun to turn, and so they went home, longing for the evening to come, when they might make the final effort.

4

Lost and Found

Tom was to dine with some relatives where he was living. When he was leaving Robert he said to him, 'Well, Bob, seven o'clock, sharp.'

'Tom, do not forget or be late. Mind, I trust you.'

'Never fear, old boy. Nothing short of death shall keep me away; but if I should happen not to turn up do not wait for me. I will be with you in spirit if I cannot be in the flesh.'

'Tom, don't talk that way. I don't know what I should do if you didn't come. It may be all a phantom we're after, but I do not like to think so. It seems so much to me.'

'All right, old man,' said Tom, cheerily, 'I shan't fail – seven o'clock,' and he was gone.

Robert was in a fever all day. He went to the church where he knew he would see Ellen, and get a smile from her in passing. He did get a smile, and a glance from her lovely dark eyes which said as plainly as if she had spoken the words with her sweet lips, 'How long you have been away; you never come to see me now.' This set Robert's heart bounding, but it increased his fever. 'How would it be,' he thought, 'if the wreck turned out a failure, and the iron box a deception? If I cannot get £100 those dark eyes will have to look sweet things to some other man; that beautiful mouth to whisper in the ears of some one who would not – could not – love her half so well as I do.'

He could not bear to meet her, so when service was over he hurried away. When she came out her eyes were beaming, for she expected to see Robert waiting for her. She looked anxiously, but could only see Mr Tomlinson, who did not rise in her favour for appearing just then.

Robert had to force himself to eat his dinner. Every morsel almost choked him, but he knew that strength was necessary for his undertaking, and so compelled himself to eat. As the hour of seven approached he began to get fidgety. He went often to the window, but could see no sign of Tom. Seven o'clock struck, but no Tom came. He began to be alarmed. Tom's words seemed to ring in his ears, 'nothing short of death shall keep me away.' He waited a little while in terrible anxiety, but then bethought him of his companion's other words, 'if I should not happen to turn up do not wait for me,' and knowing that whether he waited or no the tide would still come in all the same, and his chance of getting out the box would pass away, determined to set out alone. His determination was strengthened by the fact that the gusty wind of the morning had much increased, and sometimes swept along laden with heavy clinging mist that bespoke a great fog bank somewhere behind the wind.

Till he had reached the very shore of the 'Bull' he did not give up hopes of Tom, for he thought it just possible that he might have been delayed, and instead of increasing the delay by going home, had come on straight to the scene of operation.

There was, however, no help for it; as Tom had not come he should work alone. With misgivings he prepared himself. He left his clothes on the top of a sand-hill, put on the old ones he had brought with him, took his tools, ropes, and lantern, and set out. There was cause for alarm. The wind was rising, and it whistled in his ears as the gusts swept past. Far away in the darkness the sea was beginning to roar on the edge of the flats, and the mist came driving inland in sheets like the spume from a cataract. The water in the tidal streams as he waded across them beat against his legs and seemed cold as ice. Although now experienced in the road, he had some difficulty in finding the wreck, but at length reached it and commenced operations.

He had taken the precaution of bringing with him a second suit of old clothes and an oilskin coat. His first care was to fix the lamp where the wind could not harm it; his second, to raise the planks, and expose the interior of the wreck. Then he prepared his ropes, and, having undressed once again, went beneath the water to fasten the second rope. This he accomplished safely, and let the knot of it be on the opposite side to where the first rope was tied. He then ascended and dressed himself in all his clothes to keep him warm. He then cut off a portion in another plank, so as to expose a second one of the ship's timbers. Round this he tied one of the ropes, keeping it as taut as he could. He took a turn of the other rope round the other beam and commenced to pull. Little by little he raised the great chest from its position, and when he had raised it all he could he made that rope fast and went to the other.

By attacking the ropes alternately he raised the chest, so that he could feel from its situation that it hung suspended in the water. Then he began to shake the ropes till the chest swung like a pendulum. He held firmly both ropes, having a turn of each round its beam, and each time the weight swung he gained a little rope. So he worked on little by little, till at last, to his infinite joy, he saw the top of the box rise above the water. His excitement then changed to frenzy. His strength redoubled, and, as faster and faster the box swung, he gained more and more rope, and raised it higher and higher, till at last it ceased to rise, and he found he had reached the maximum height attainable by this means. As, however, it was now nearly up he detached a long timber, and using it as a lever, slowly, after repeated failures, prized up the chest through the gap till it reached the bottom of the ship, and then, toppling over, fell with a dull thud upon the sand.

With a cry of joy Robert jumped down after it, but in jumping lit on the edge of it and wrenched his ankle so severely that when he rose up and attempted to stand on it it gave way under him, and he fell again. He managed, however, to crawl out of the hulk, and reached his lantern. The wind by this time was blowing louder and louder, and the mist was gathering in white masses, and sweeping by, mingled with sleet. In endeavouring to guard the lantern from the wind he slipped once more on the wet timbers, and fell down, striking his leg against the sharp edge of the chest. So severe was the pain that for a few moments he became almost insensible, and when he recovered his senses found he was quite unable to stir.

The lantern had fallen in a pool of water, and had of

course gone out. It was a terrible situation, and Robert's
heart sank within him, as well it might, as he thought of
what was to come. The wind was rapidly rising to a storm,
and swept by him, laden with the deadly mist in fierce gusts.
The roaring of the tide grew nearer and nearer, and louder
and louder. Overhead was a pall of darkness, save when in
the leaden winter sky some white pillar of mist swept
onward like an embodied spirit of the storm. All the past
began to crowd Robert's memory, and more especially the
recent past. He thought of his friend's words – 'Nothing short
of death shall keep me away,' and so full of dismal shadows,
and forms of horror was all the air, that he could well fancy
that Tom was dead, and that his spirit was circling round
him, wailing through the night. Then again, arose the memory of his dream, and his very heart stood still, as he thought
of how awfully it had been fulfilled. There he now lay; not in
a dream, but in reality, beside a ship on a waste of desert
sand. Beside him lay a chest such as he had seen in his
dreams, and, as before, death seemed flapping his giant
wings over his head. Strange horrors seemed to gather round
him, borne on the wings of the blast. His father, whom he
had never seen, he felt to be now beside him. All the dead
that he had ever known circled round him in a weird dance.
As the stormy gusts swept by, he heard amid their screams
the lugubrious tolling of bells; bells seemed to be all around
him; whichever way he turned he heard his knell. All forms
were gathered there, as in his dreams – all save Ellen. But
hark! even as the thought flashed across his brain; his ears
seemed to hear her voice as one hears in a dream. He tried to
cry out, but was so overcome by cold, that he could barely
hear his own voice. He tried to rise, but in vain, and then,
overcome by pain and excitement, and disappointed hope, he
became insensible.

Was his treasure-hunting to end thus?

As Mr Stedman and Ellen were sitting down to tea that
evening, Arthur Tomlinson being the only other guest, a
hurried knock came to the cottage door. The little servant
came into the room a moment after, looking quite scared,
and holding a letter in her hand. She came over to Ellen and

faltered out, 'Oh, please, miss, there's a man from the hospital, and he says as how you're to open the letter and to come
at once; it's a matter of life and death.'

Ellen grew white as a sheet, and stood up quickly, trembling as she opened the letter. Mr Stedman rose up, too.
Arthur Tomlinson sat still, and glared at the young servant
till, thinking she had done something wrong, she began to
cry. The letter was from the doctor of the hospital, written
for Tom, and praying her to come at once, as the latter had
something to tell her of the greatest import to one for whom
he was sure she would do much. She immediately ran and
put on her cloak, and asked her father to come with her.

'Surely you won't go?' said Tomlinson.

'What else should I do?' she asked, scornfully; 'I must
apologise for leaving you, unless you will come with us.'

'No, thank you; I am not a philanthropist.'

In half an hour they had reached the hospital, and had
heard Tom's story. Poor fellow, when hurrying home to
Robert, he had been knocked down by a car and had his leg
broken. As soon as he could he had sent word to Ellen, for he
feared for Robert being out alone at the wreck, knowing how
chilled he had been on the previous night, and he thought
that if any one would send him aid Ellen would.

No sooner had the story been told, and Ellen had understood the danger Robert was in, than with her father she
hurried off to the 'Bull.'

They got a car with some difficulty, and drove as fast as
the horse could go, and arriving at the 'Bull,' called to the
coastguard-station. None of the coastguards had seen Robert
that evening, but on learning of his possible danger all that
were in the station at once turned out. They wrapped Ellen
and her father in oilskins, and, taking lanterns and ropes,
set out for the wreck. They all knew its position, and went as
straight for it as they could, and, as they crossed the sand-
hills, found Robert's clothes. At this they grew very grave.
They wanted to leave Ellen on the shore, but she refused
point blank. By this time the storm was blowing wildly, and
the roaring of the sea being borne on the storm was frightful
to hear. The tidal streams were running deeper than usual,
and there was some difficulty in crossing to the wreck.

In the mist the men lost their way a little, and could not tell exactly how far to go. They shouted as loudly as they could, but there was no reply. Ellen's terror grew into despair. She too, shouted, although fearing that to shout in the teeth of such a wind her woman's voice would be of no avail. However, her clear soprano rang out louder than the hoarse shouts of the sturdy sailors, and cleft the storm like a wedge. Twice or thrice she cried, 'Robert, Robert, Robert,' but still there was no reply. Suddenly she stopped, and, bending her head, cried joyfully, 'He is there, he is there; I hear his voice,' and commenced running as fast as she could through the darkness towards the raging sea. The coastguards called out to her to mind where she was going, and followed her with the lanterns as fast as they could run.

When they came up with her they found her sitting on an iron chest close to the wreck, with Robert resting on her knees, and his head pillowed on her breast. He had opened his eyes, and was faintly whispering, 'Ellen, my love, my love. It was to win you I risked my life.'

She bent and kissed him, even there among rough sailors, and then, amid the storm, she whispered softly, 'It was not risked in vain.'